Kathi

"I have a letter for you..."

Kate regarded the soldier. He was daringly, breathtakingly handsome—the reason a woman should leave home and look at all men before settling down to just one. Because there might be a man as handsome as Kyle for every woman.

She read the letter, absorbing its words more out of curiosity than any real interest. She'd always been more friend than lover to her fiancé.

"He's a screwup," Kyle spat out. "Enchanting, funny and nice, but a screwup nonetheless. I'll make him pay for this in my own sort of way."

Kyle was close to her, his breath warm on her neck, and she breathed deeply of his masculine scent. Without forethought, Kate caressed his cheek. He didn't flinch. She tilted her head... parted her lips.

For the first time in her life, Kate was doing something shocking and sexy, daring and crazy. Something not at all sensible or responsible or right.

She was going to give the town something to talk about.

ABOUT THE AUTHOR

Bestselling author Vivian Leiber lives in what she calls an "itsy-bitsy town" in the heart of Illinois corn country. She loves small-town life—thrills to the Fourth of July parade that usually has more people watching than marching, delights in the local winter carnival when Santa Claus stops in for a quick visit, volunteers every June to work the nursery school's children's fair and coaches boys' soccer two seasons a year. Believing that every woman has a wondrous story about how she found love, Vivian tries to write just one of those special stories at a time.

Books by Vivian Leiber

HARLEQUIN AMERICAN ROMANCE
576—BABY MAKES NINE
640—BLUE-JEANED PRINCE
655—MARRYING NICKY
672—A MILLION-DOLLAR MAN

HARLEQUIN INTRIGUE
416—HIS KIND OF TROUBLE

Don't miss any of our special offers. Write to us at the following address for information on our newest releases.

Harlequin Reader Service
U.S.: 3010 Walden Ave., P.O. Box 1325, Buffalo, NY 14269
Canadian: P.O. Box 609, Fort Erie, Ont. L2A 5X3

Vivian Leiber

ALWAYS A HERO

Harlequin Books

TORONTO • NEW YORK • LONDON
AMSTERDAM • PARIS • SYDNEY • HAMBURG
STOCKHOLM • ATHENS • TOKYO • MILAN
MADRID • WARSAW • BUDAPEST • AUCKLAND

This book is dedicated to the Eastmans

ISBN 0-373-16686-9

ALWAYS A HERO

Copyright © 1997 by Arlynn Leiber Presser.

Chapter One

Kyle Reeves pulled his camouflage-painted all-terrain vehicle to a halt in the dusty cul-de-sac of the Two for the Road tin shack. Ignoring the cheerful invitations of the working girls, he threw a generous fistful of change into the shrieking swarm of street urchins that had arisen from the dusty street.

"There's more of that if I come out and my car hasn't been touched," he shouted as the coins fell into eager little hands, knowing at least one of the Colomban children would be sufficiently fluent in English—or the international language of money—to understand him.

The Two for the Road's neon sign was off in deference to the broiling midday sun, but the bar's garish charm wasn't otherwise compromised. The roof was shingled with orange, purple and blue tin, and lemon yellow and crimson batik curtains faintly vibrated in its two windows. A hand-painted sign posted on the teak doorway promised all the base delights any red-blooded man would want.

American whiskey, German beer, Japanese saki—

and lots of women who could make a man forget he was far from home. Or maybe make him feel good he was halfway around the world from whatever he'd left behind.

The island of Sri Lanka, off the southern tip of India, had been Kyle's home for nearly twelve years. Not that he stayed much at the Pidurutalagal Mountain cardamom and black tea plantation he had bought from a retired exporter. Kyle had never needed or wanted the security of a home. As long as he had his duffel bag and his next assignment, he was content. Happiness wasn't something he thought about all that often.

But if he had been asked about it, he would have admitted that at this moment he wasn't happy. At the end of his enlistment, he had one last duty run to make: Fly into Washington, pick up a medal for an antiterrorist mission he had successfully completed two months before, shake hands with the current occupant of the White House and debrief a couple of desks from the Pentagon.

The trip was one Kyle made every year or so and he didn't like it any better now than he did the first time he'd had to do it. Heading stateside for recognition of doing his job was the only part of his work for the Special Forces Rapid Reaction unit that he didn't enjoy. He was a tough, proud, strong man who had completed hundreds of dangerous missions in the jungles of Asia, the deserts of the Middle East, even the tundra of Russia. He had faced down every enemy, rescued every hostage, had never left a buddy behind.

But he hated dress uniform, considered politicians and cockroaches to be from the same species and he wasn't comfortable with the forced familiarity of the officers' club parties he would be obligated to attend. The desks in Washington too often forgot the grisly realities of the battles they sent young men to fight.

He shoved open the heavy teak door, pulled off his aviator sunglasses and squinted his eyes to adjust to the light. Or rather, the dark. He ran a quick hand through his hair, newly shorn in preparation for his trip stateside.

Inside, a ceiling fan stirred cool air heavy with the scent of stale smoke and sweat. On a small round stage a bored, naked woman in white spike-heeled sandals danced for two inebriated customers.

Kyle settled onto a bar stool. A tall, patrician bartender with round wire rimmed glasses and a thin face was slicing lemons and limes.

"Hiya, Parker," Kyle said. "Too early for beer— make it a soda."

Drink produced, Parker pointed to the stage. "Says her name's Tequila," he said. "She's from Brazil. I think she has potential."

Kyle didn't turn around. "You said you had a favor to ask."

"Oh, yeah." Parker bit his lip. "I'm supposed to get married in three weeks."

Kyle put his drink down. "Congratulations," he said.

And he meant it. He had seen the picture of Parker's fiancée in the bar's back office. The picture had been oddly affecting. Was that envy that flickered across his emotional radar screen?

No way, Kyle countered mentally. He had never been the marrying kind. He'd seen many a fine soldier give up the life just for a woman. Besides, he'd never give up his freedom. And he'd never felt possessive enough about any woman to ask her to be his.

"Save the congrats," Parker said. He leaned over the bar. "I'm breaking it off."

Kyle stared at Parker. He thought of the picture of the fiancée—a redhead. He remembered a blur of freckles and an earnest smile.

From what little Parker had told him, Parker's fiancée was the perfect woman to have on your arm at, say, a church social or a preschool graduation. A perfect woman to bear your children, keep them on the straight and narrow and host a nice Sunday dinner for your folks. Not the type who would know how to give a man a mindblowing massage with her feet.

"Why are you breaking up with her?" Kyle asked neutrally. A man didn't inquire too much about another man's business—but Parker looked as if he was itching to talk.

"I can't go home." Parker sighed dramatically. "I like it here too much—it's not anything like my hometown. Winnetka's just a group of houses surrounded by cornfields. Lots and lots of cornfields.''

"Sounds awful." Kyle reluctantly thought of the Kentucky farming town he had once called home. Tobacco instead of corn, but the same idea.

"It *is* awful. And Kate's not going to leave her family to come out here," he said, glancing up at Tequila.

Kyle didn't follow his gaze—maybe he was getting old, but gyrating working girls didn't excite him too much anymore.

"Her not coming here is probably a good thing," Parker mused. "She wouldn't appreciate the atmosphere."

"Then she must not really love you."

"I guess," Parker agreed hastily. Too hastily. "But there's also family to consider. Mine as well as hers."

Kyle narrowed his eyes at Parker. He sensed Parker had something he wasn't saying. But Kyle had survived for thirty years with a very simple philosophy of not getting involved in other people's business. He wasn't about to change now. Especially for Parker. He had gotten involved once in Parker's life. Once had been enough.

He nursed his soda while Parker switched off the music and told Tequila to take a break—her audience of two had passed out at their table. Then Parker leaned forward so that his nose nearly touched Kyle's.

"I have a letter I want you to mail from Washington," he whispered.

Parker held out the envelope.

Kyle recoiled.

He had been asked many times for favors when he went stateside. He did some, ducked others that were too involved, too risky or potentially illegal.

But this one was too emotionally heavy.

"You're breaking it off by letter?" he asked.

Parker nodded. "And I want it to have a D.C. postmark so she doesn't come around here looking for me. Kyle, I've tried to be gentle."

"Three weeks' notice?"

"Yeah, it's probably a little overdue. If you mail it from D.C. the first day you get there, she'll know within two weeks of the date. She probably won't get her deposit back on the hall or be able to return her dress—but she'll still have some time to cancel the honeymoon plans and the caterer."

"Why couldn't you have done this a little earlier? Maybe even in person? That's how a man should do it."

"I'm a coward."

"We both know that already," Kyle said blandly.

The two men looked down at the bar. They didn't have to talk about it—though, even years later, the memories were still vivid. It wasn't something Kyle thought about often, but he imagined it haunted Parker. Coming close to death had a way of haunting a man.

"You know what the Chinese say?" Parker asked.

"No. And I don't want to know. Because somehow I think you're going to tell me that the Chinese have a saying that makes it impossible for me to refuse you. And Parker, I'm refusing. Saving your life once was enough—saving your butt on account of a woman is too much."

"The Chinese say that if you save a man's life, that man belongs to you," Parker said, ignoring Kyle's protest. "That means you own me, Kyle, and I'm telling you, you've got to get me out of this wedding. I don't want to marry the girl next door. I don't want to live in a small town, the same town as my parents and their parents before them lived in. I don't want to grow up and have kids and do any of that stuff. I want to stay here. And continue to serve you. You, Kyle, the guy who owns me."

"I don't think the Chinese wise men had you in mind when they said that," Kyle said dryly. "And I don't have any interest in owning you, Parker. You're more trouble than a poodle and less interesting than a goldfish."

"Just take the envelope."

Kyle shook his head. "No, Parker, I can't," Kyle said, and he added a stern warning. "I'd never get myself into the situation you're in, but if I did, at least I'd have the guts to face the woman myself."

"You wouldn't if the woman was Kate," Parker said, gulping.

"And what makes her so scary?" Kyle asked,

thinking that the photograph had made her seem as wholesome as apple pie, the flag and Mother's Day all rolled into one. What was Parker afraid of?

"She's not a scary woman," Parker admitted. "She's a good woman. And that's exactly the problem."

"Scared of a good woman, huh? If that's your problem, buddy, it's all yours. Put the envelope away and call her yourself. Or, better yet, fly there and tell her yourself. If you act like a man about it, Parker, you'll feel a lot better."

KATE LODGE WINCED as the seamstress stuck pins into her waist.

"Kate, I used to have the same problem you're having now," Mrs. Maguire said, managing to speak without swallowing the five pins she held between her teeth. "Too skinny. Just too skinny I was. Then the doctors ordered me to drink a milk shake every day. Oh, how I hated those milk shakes. Chocolate milk shakes, vanilla milk shakes, strawberry milk shakes. Ugh!"

"So then what happened?"

"I got addicted to milk shakes, and look at me now!"

Kate leaned over the layers of tulle and silk that draped around the not-at-all skinny seamstress.

"Don't move," Mrs. Maguire commanded. "I've still got to pin around those tiny hips of yours. Fact is, Kate, if you keep losing weight, I'll never get this dress finished in time for the wedding."

"Sorry. I'll drink some milk shakes."

"I sure understand wedding jitters," Mrs. Maguire mused with the authority of being Winnetka's finest seamstress specializing in weddings for over twenty years. "And you especially. No wonder you're nervous—but I assure you it's going to be the nicest wedding Winnetka's ever seen. It's just like a fairy tale—the town's hero returning from the fields of battle to marry his beautiful princess who has waited so long for him."

Kate winced as the word *hero* was said without irony or sarcasm. Parker Cabot IV was Winnetka's greatest hero. It was true, she supposed. Children in the neighborhood pretended to be him when they played war. His face appeared several times a year in the *Winnetka Talk* newspaper. His name was invoked when discussions turned to international politics. Folks talked about how he had given so much to his country, and everyone agreed he deserved every honor that would be heaped upon him when he came back this very day—just in time to lead the town's Fourth of July parade tomorrow morning.

A hero, everyone said. They must be right.

But was she a princess?

Kate looked into the full-length mirror that had been brought into her bedroom for the fitting with Mrs. Maguire. She didn't often look at herself more than to establish that her lipstick was in the right place. But now, required to stand absolutely still for Mrs. Maguire's second fitting, she inspected herself more carefully.

And she didn't see any princess.

She saw a tall, skinny—maybe too skinny—woman with coppery red hair that erupted in corkscrew curls. Green eyes that, if she tilted her chin a different way, turned blue in the sunlight filtering through the wispy lace bedroom curtains. A pale rose-colored mouth that was too full.

And there were freckles. Far too many freckles on her nose, across her shoulders... And, if she had yanked off her gown, she knew she would see freckles across her pale stomach and all the way down her legs. She even had freckles on her toes. Kate had spent her teens trying to get rid of them with lemon juice, creams from the drugstore, milk baths, baking soda pastes, even epsom salts. Now, at the brink of thirty, she had given up.

Not her idea of a princess.

And she wasn't sure if she was ready for the boy next door who was now a revered hero. Sometimes her stomach fluttered at the thought of the brave and fierce things Parker wrote about in his letters home—he was modest, but generally forthcoming about his exploits on behalf of the Special Forces unit that kept him somewhere in Southeast Asia.

He wasn't able to tell her exactly where he was—security reasons, he explained. And Kate hadn't seen him in—could it really be?—two years. But that was because the training was so intense, Parker wrote, that the morale of the unit couldn't be broken by long absences. Or weekends. Phone calls were even a problem.

She wasn't sure if she was ready to pledge her life to Parker, but their wedding was a bare week and a half away. No time now for second thoughts. Besides, there was no reason for second thoughts.

Kate had lived next door to Parker all her life. Had played in the same sandbox, ate next to him at the school cafeteria, had shared her first fumbling kiss with him, had made love to him and to him alone—and that was all right, even if she had been left with a strange sensation that this making love couldn't possibly be the thing that drove perfectly normal people wild.

She loved Parker. Would always love him in a way that was probably more affection than passion, more devotion than sensual hunger, a love more comfortable than bunny slippers on a cold winter night.

And the question of whether she was in love seemed almost juvenile compared to the larger questions of when and how they would marry, raise a family, watch over their parents as they retired. Especially Parker's parents, who both had been suffering from health problems for years.

Besides, Kate didn't think Parker felt any differently toward her. She figured she wasn't the kind of woman to inspire grand passion.

"Kate, this woven silk is so well-made, it deserves a perfect fit," Mrs. Maguire said. "My prescription is one milk shake a—"

Suddenly, from downstairs, Kate's mother screamed.

THE FIRST THING about any assignment is knowing when to pull out. Now was definitely that time, Kyle thought.

"What's happened to Parker?" Mrs. Lodge shrieked as a follow-up to her ear-blasting scream upon opening the door to the white Victorian farmhouse. "What's happened to our Parker?"

With a sharp, pincerlike hold on his arm that would have done the bravest guerrilla fighter proud, she dragged Kyle into the yellow wallpapered foyer. It smelled of fresh bread and vanilla and sported a console with flowers cascading from a white milk pitcher.

At that moment, he would have traded his soul to be back on the dusty streets of Colombo. Anywhere but here in Winnetka, Illinois.

"Nothing's happened to Parker," he said calmly.

He pried one finger off of his arm, but Mrs. Lodge countered with a two-handed assault.

"It was in South America, wasn't it?" she demanded, eyes narrowing behind her bifocals. "It was those drug cartel people, right?"

Drug cartel people? Kyle wondered. "No, Parker's fine and he's never been to South—" Suddenly Kyle remembered that Parker hadn't wanted his fiancée to know exactly where he was.

Kyle hated being deceptive with civilians—those people who thought the world worked because of values like decency, honesty and good citizenship, people who didn't know it was men like himself who insured their safety.

And he certainly didn't want to lie to the mother of his friend's fiancée. *That*, he thought, must come under a special category of terrible.

"Parker's... He's still in..." Kyle struggled trying to gracefully extricate himself from the situation.

"Oh, I gotcha now!" Mrs. Lodge zipped her fingers over her lips and smiled conspiratorially. "Security reasons. You can't tell me, but you can count on my discretion."

Puzzled, he nearly asked what she meant but his attention faltered. At first, all he could see was a delicate pale hand on the banister, and white, billowing clouds of silk. And then, coming down the final curve of steps, *she* emerged—her face glowing with piquant concern, her eyes sparkling like fiery blue-green opals.

The fiancée.

Ex-fiancée.

Kate.

"Mother, what's wrong?"

Kyle opened his mouth in amazement. She was everything like her picture—all the parts were there. The red curls. The slender nose. The tiny freckles that made her look like a spokeswoman for the Girl Scouts. And yet, she was nothing like her picture. The camera hadn't captured the truth of her. She was a beauty. Not like Parker's newest talents at the bar. No, she was a beauty like only an innocent could be beautiful. And a man couldn't lie to her without feeling like a dog.

He cursed Parker and his own internal weaknesses

that had made him vulnerable to Parker's begging and manipulative charm. He should have carried Parker to the tarmac at Colombo and thrown him on a C-130 transport jet, made him come home and face her himself.

Better, he should have told Parker that he didn't believe in Chinese sayings popped off by American cowards, and he should have added that Parker could work this one out on his own.

Definitely time to get out, Kyle thought, looking for an escape route. But the cab he had arrived in had just pulled away.

It was time to reevaluate his options. Fast!

A good and beautiful woman could be very dangerous to a man like him.

Chapter Two

"It was the uniform that did it," Mrs. Lodge told the Cabots. *Damn regulations,* Kyle thought.

"I figured the lieutenant here was on official business. You know, when they send someone to break the news? When they have terrible news for the next of kin."

Her listeners nodded solemnly.

Kyle was stuck in Parker Cabot's childhood home, drinking tea out of a bone china teacup served with a saucer and a pale linen napkin, sitting on an upholstered chair that was just the right size for a doll—all because of his dress blues.

Mrs. Cabot pushed a tray in his direction. It was piled high with tiny triangular pieces of crustless bread that contained, he had been assured, cucumber, watercress and cream cheese.

Not a man's kind of sandwich at all.

He shook his head.

Parker Cabot's fiancée—make that soon-to-be-ex-fiancée—was pinned into an unfinished wedding dress. She stared at him from a love seat across the room.

Unreadable expression.

Eyes narrowed.

Kyle liked to know what other people were thinking—gave him an advantage.

She didn't give him any satisfaction on that score.

He wondered if she had figured out why he was here or if she was staring at him because he was committing some little known but serious breach of etiquette.

He looked down at his lap—napkin in place right on his knee. He looked at his cup—teaspoon on the rim of the saucer, lemon slice floating in the center of the pale liquid.

Nope, didn't seem to be doing much wrong.

Still, he placed the teacup and saucer on the coffee table. Safer that way.

"So I screamed," Mrs. Lodge continued. "I must have sounded like a lunatic, but I thought for sure something had happened to our dear Parker."

Our dear Parker.

Kyle looked around the room. Parker had a lot of "owners" above and beyond being "owned" by Kyle.

There were Mr. and Mrs. Lodge, who now sat side by side like matching white-haired bookends on the couch in front of the fireplace.

There was the delicate yet impressive Mrs. Cabot who fussed over her tray set and now produced a plate of dainty cookies. There was also Parker's father, Mr. Cabot, who sat in the doll-size chair flanking Kyle's and asked Kyle on several occasions how he liked working with General Eisenhower, as though there had been no other generals since.

And a Mrs. Maguire, whose relationship to the parties hadn't been made clear to Kyle but who possessed the singular talent of being able to drink tea with a mouthful of pins lodged between her teeth.

And, of course, there was Kate.

Good, beautiful Kate.

Kyle felt Parker's envelope burning a hole in the pocket of his jacket. If Parker hadn't wheedled him so much, he wouldn't have brought it back from Colombo. If Kyle hadn't been kept so busy by official handlers, he would have remembered to mail it. And if he hadn't felt so bad when he found the letter in his duffel, he wouldn't have persuaded the pilot of a C-130 naval transport jet to let him hitch a ride to Chicago. He wouldn't be stuck here in Parker's living room, doing Parker's dirty work.

He glanced at Kate and wondered if she'd cry. But she didn't look like the kind of woman who cried. Ever. Women with strong, square jaws didn't do that sort of thing. And in the midst of her delicate beauty, she had a jaw that told a man he'd better act his best.

Maybe Parker was better off without her.

"You didn't tell us your name," Kate asked, interrupting her mother's description of how her heart irregularities had acted up when Kyle appeared at the door. "What's your name, soldier?"

"Lieutenant Kyle Reeves, ma'am," Kyle replied. "I'm just a friend of Parker's."

There was an audible gasp. Even Kate was taken aback, her face flushing bright crimson. Kyle wondered what he had said.

"We know who you are," Mrs. Cabot said gently, patting his sleeve.

"We know you probably don't want to talk about it," Mrs. Lodge ventured. "We understand you might feel…shy about the whole incident. But Parker really cares for you."

"We all know the whole story," Mr. Cabot assured Kyle, staring at him through the wrong part of his bifocals. "I can see that you'd be very close to Parker after…after what happened."

"Leave the poor man alone," Mr. Lodge warned. "He's been through so much."

Everyone in the room stared at Kyle.

"What happened?" Kyle asked cautiously.

"What happened is our dear Parker saved your life!" Mrs. Maguire squeaked, nearly swallowing her pins.

"SAVED MY LIFE? Saved my life!" Kyle groaned, slamming his hand against the porch column. He released a string of unrepeatable oaths. Then he noticed Kate, who slid into the wicker settee behind him. "Sorry, ma'am, I don't ordinarily swear around…ladies."

"I'm sure you don't," Kate said smoothly. She wasn't sure she liked being called ma'am and she was positive that, at this moment, she didn't want to be called a lady.

The word sounded way too prissy.

She smoothed the voluminous skirt of her gown. It wasn't meant for sitting in, but she supposed that the gown didn't matter now. She wasn't going to sit or stand in it much longer.

She wondered vaguely if it was time to call the caterer and if he would agree to take the reception food to the church homeless shelter. The flowers could go to the seniors' home. Unfortunately, the Moose Lodge would probably want to keep the deposit on the hall, but she could hardly blame them.

"I take it you have a different version of the story of how Parker saved your life?" she asked.

She regarded the soldier closely. Oh, he was handsome. Daringly, breathtakingly handsome. He was the reason a woman should leave home right after college and go to the four corners of the world and look at all the men, all of them, before she settled down to just one. Because there might be a man this handsome for every woman.

Kate ached inside. She would never in her life have a man like this one to call her own—however briefly.

Then she wondered why she wasn't mourning for her wedding to Parker. After all, she knew what was coming, had figured it out by the way Lieutenant Reeves avoided her eyes from the moment they'd met. But how come Parker's betrayal didn't break her heart?

"I have a letter for you from Parker," Kyle said stiffly, pulling an envelope from inside the jacket of his uniform. He held it out to her.

After she took it, he stepped away from her, gazing with apparent, discreet interest at the lawn sprinkler drifting back and forth, showering the sidewalk one second and the closely shorn grass the next.

Kate noticed Kyle never answered whether Parker's account of his heroism was accurate or whether he had a different version of the story.

She wondered what he thought about all the medals Parker had sent home and which the Cabots had just now displayed for Kyle. He hadn't said a word, just crimsoned once, drawing a ruddy, rugged tone to his cheeks. And then had excused himself to the porch for a smoke—and Kate noticed now he didn't smoke.

She opened the letter.

Might as well get it over with.

She hoped she wouldn't make a fool of herself and cry—although her tears would be more about the lost opportunities of her life than about Parker himself. Kyle looked like the type of man who would comfort a teary-eyed woman, even if she wasn't the sort of woman a man would want to comfort.

The few occasions she'd cried, she didn't look pale and tragic and in need of masculine reassurance. Instead she ended up blotchy red, puffy-cheeked and, if she wore mascara, it left a big, black mess on her cheeks.

But Lieutenant Reeves would do the right thing and produce a handkerchief and maybe even a solicitous hug and she'd feel pity oozing from him. That she couldn't bear.

She read the words, cringing at Parker's bold statements. He had left her holding the bag—although she had let him, she knew. She had never protested his joining the army.

It hadn't been his fault. He didn't know she would have stayed in Winnetka forever in order to care for her parents. Adding Parker's parents to the list of responsibilities wasn't a stretch—even without a wedding ring—since the two families were always close in ways that the words *next-door neighbors* couldn't begin to describe their relationship. He didn't know he could have broken up with her in a more straightforward way. And perhaps she was a fool to have waited for him to finally do it the way he did.

She finished reading the letter, absorbing its words more out of curiosity than any real interest. And then she folded the tissue-light sheets of paper and neatly slid them into the envelope.

She was grateful for one thing.

She wouldn't cry.

"I'm sorry to bring this to you," Kyle said, and when he turned toward her, she could see in his hand that patronizing handkerchief. "He asked me to mail it, and I reluctantly agreed. But I got tied up in Washington and I realized that if I mailed it now you might not have enough time to make appropriate arrangements.''

"I'm not planning a funeral. I'm just canceling a wedding."

"Sorry, ma'am. I didn't mean to—"

"I'm proud of him," Kate interrupted firmly. "I'm proud of the sacrifice he's making for his country. He's a hero."

She said the words deliberately. She could tell this man didn't suffer fools, had probably felt used and abused by Parker quite enough for one day and no doubt would give Parker a dressing down when he returned to whatever country Parker had come to call home.

"What sacrifice?" Kyle demanded, handkerchief abruptly shoved back into his pocket.

Kate took a deep breath wondering how far she'd have to push to get what she wanted. Kyle seemed to be an honorable man, but she would need to shove him toward one particular dishonor—ratting on a buddy to confirm everything she had already reluctantly guessed.

In the past years she had wondered about Parker's exploits. Now this letter and the appearance of Lieutenant Kyle Reeves tipped her over the edge, and crystalized all her suspicions. But she needed confirmation.

"Well he's had to go deep undercover for the Special Forces, joining a newly formed rapid reaction unit." She answered in a sort of soft Southern drawl. "That's why he's not coming home to marry me."

"Parker wrote that?"

He was clearly incredulous. Almost ready to explode. Kate nearly had him, nearly had the truth confirmed for her. However much it hurt, she had to know for sure. Not so she could ruin Parker's reputation, which she could, but she wouldn't because she did still care for him. No, she had to know the truth so that in the coming years she would have no doubts. About herself. About the wrongness of the marriage now just averted.

"Yes, he's going to head a new rapid reaction force for several years," she said, with what she thought might be just the right touch of wistfulness. "Won't be able to communicate at all. Security has to be kept very tight. It's quite a sacrifice for our country, but he hopes that I'll understand that he's fighting for a better world for me and all the other people of our country. Aren't you proud of him?"

"He's laid it on a little thick, even for Parker," Kyle muttered, shaking his head.

Kate agreed silently. "Anyhow, he says he must release me from this engagement because it's unfair to me," she added, hoping this would be enough to tip the lieutenant right over the edge.

"So you'll...carry on bravely?" Kyle asked, turning to study her closely. "Finding another man, but remembering Parker fondly and with deep respect?"

In her openmouthed admiration of Kyle, she forgot her strategy of drawing him out. She had nearly missed the trap. He had laid his more effectively than she had laid hers.

If she gave him any hint that she was going to forgive Parker and get on with her life, he could walk away. He'd be angry, perhaps, and ready to light into Parker when he got back to wherever he called home—although Parker had always been charming enough to diffuse anyone's anger.

Still, if she hinted that she wasn't completely devastated by this, Kyle would walk away from her, thinking she believed she had been sacrificed for patriotism—not because her fiancé was a coward and a charmer and a sweet-talking boy. A lady sacrificed for love of country preserves her pride and honor—and Kyle's sense of honor obviously required that he only leave her with both.

The stakes had risen just a little bit, but she had to see it through.

"No, I don't think I can continue," she said dramatically, wondering if she could get herself to cry if she had to. She'd have to live with his pity, and oh! how that would rankle, but he was a strong-willed man. She would simply have to be stronger, with the only weapons available to her. She sniffed lightly.

"He's not worth it," he said quietly, clearly hoping the single admission would be enough.

"Oh, but Parker Cabot IV is worth it! He's a hero and there aren't many heroes left in this world."

"You don't believe that."

"But I do," she lied coolly.

"Look, he wants you to make a new life," Kyle said, switching tactics. "You have to forget him— have a good cry and then get on with your life. Make his sacrifice worthwhile."

He was improvising now, and Kate saw he was good on his feet. Very good at seeing the escape hatch and diving for it. This was a man who had gotten himself out of trouble before. And knew how to do it with style.

But he'd never been in trouble with Kate before.

"I don't know how I can go on," Kate said, trying to make her lower lip tremble. She sniffed a bit more loudly than she had the first time.

"He'd want you to."

"I don't think I can."

"You're going to cry? Because you don't look like the kind of woman who would cry."

He certainly had that right. Dependable, level-headed, sensible Kate. It was a mantra of Winnetka—you could count on Kate to weather every storm, every tragedy, every terrible situation with a dry eye, a clear mind and a cool perspective.

Crying? That wasn't what people expected from Kate—it wasn't the kind of thing Kate ever did.

She'd plan how to make sure no one else got hurt by this. Pay the caterer, comfort the families, return the wedding presents, call the high school to tell them that counting on Parker to coach the football team to victory this year wasn't in the cards.

Still…she'd like to go back to her house, slam

the doors a few times, throw a couple of vases—make that pillows—and then have a real good long selfish cry.

Not for Parker, who was no doubt enjoying himself somewhere and didn't need her tears. No, she'd love to cry for the way she had barely noticed that her life was drifting away and that she didn't want to be dependable, sensible or even levelheaded all the time. She wanted to be in love, have a life, cause a stir. Instead, she had waited in vain for Parker.

In New York, even in Chicago, thirty wasn't old—thirty was still blind dates and whirlwind courtships and throwing caution to the wind. Here in Winnetka, thirty was having the kids start junior high and saving for a family vacation.

For a single woman in this small town, thirty was a spinster, which Kate had just become. She hated the word, but recognized the reality.

"I'm not going to cry," she conceded, but then saw her opening. "But I'm never going to be the same. I'll never marry. Or have children. Or…give myself to another man."

He swallowed hard.

She wondered if she had gone too far. Especially that last part. Sounded way too dramatic, didn't it?

"Damn it, Miss Lodge, he's not a hero."

"Oh, really?"

You're reeling him in now, don't get impatient and blow it, she thought. *Don't show any excitement, not a touch of "thought so"—just let him finish his thoughts. Out loud.*

"No, he's not a hero," Kyle said, crouching down in front of her. "Those medals the Cabots proudly display in the sitting room aren't his. They're mine. I don't give a damn about that sort of thing, and I had no idea what Parker did with them when he asked me for them. I certainly didn't know he was mailing them home with narratives about his fictional exploits."

"Oh, dear."

"It gets worse, ma'am. As for that story he told you about saving my life, he didn't do it. Not even close. He's a coward, although a charming one, and I've known it from the moment I met him."

I think I knew that, too, Kate thought to herself. But she kept her eyes wide and unblinking, she didn't want to distract the lieutenant. As much as it hurt, she had to hear everything. So she would never have any doubts in the long, cold nights that spread out in front of her.

"He's a screwup," Kyle spat out. "An enchanting and funny screwup, a really nice screwup. But a screwup nonetheless. He barely managed to get out of the army without being court-martialed for laziness."

Kate gasped. It was worse than she had ever imagined!

But the lieutenant wasn't finished yet.

"And he's spent the last few years running a gin joint in Sri Lanka that's not particularly profitable and is very much not the sort of place a…lady such as yourself should go. So don't even think of going after him, and rest assured I'll make him pay for all this in my own sort of way."

He was close to her, his breath warm on her cheek, and she breathed deeply of his scent of citrus and something masculine. Without forethought she caressed his cheek, tormenting herself with its smoothness. He didn't flinch. She leaned forward, wincing as Mrs. Maguire's pins raked across her back. She opened her mouth, feeling the July heat touch her tongue. All she had to do was tilt her head, offer herself to him. It would be charity for him, but a wondrous memory for her.

For the first time in her life, Kate was contemplating doing something shocking and sexy and daring and crazy. Something not at all sensible or responsible or dependable or right.

She was really going to give Winnetka something to talk about—assuming Winnetka ever found out.

And Winnetka, being a small town, always found out.

Chapter Three

But it was ten o'clock on a bright summer morning. Sultry and passionate things just didn't happen on the Cabots' front porch, on any Winnetka porch, at this time of day.

Besides, Kate was Kate.

And, as always, her first thought was of duty, her duty to her parents and the Cabots. They would be shocked and confused if she gave in to her impulse. They would regard it as a betrayal against Parker.

And if she explained why she was acting in such an outrageous and peculiar fashion, they would be devastated by the truth about Parker.

Maybe they didn't need to know the truth. Or, at least, all the truth all at one time. Obviously, she'd have to admit that he wasn't coming home today. And the wedding... She'd have to cancel that.

But the rest? It was so shocking that perhaps it was better to wait until the town's focus had shifted, until the Cabots were more settled with the notion that Parker wasn't coming home.

In any event, she had to get rid of Kyle Reeves,

right now before he shot his mouth off to anyone else. Before she lost all sense and kissed him.

She stood abruptly. Confused, he scrambled to his feet, placing his hand on the soft fold of her hip.

They both looked down at his hand as if it were a red-hot iron about to burn Mrs. Maguire's precious silk.

He jerked away. "I'm so sorry, ma'am," he said, uncertainty about her seductive intentions creeping into his voice. "About my behavior. About Parker. I'm telling you, I'll rake him over the coals but good on your behalf when I get back to Sri Lanka."

"Don't bother," Kate said. She swept her gown up into a barely manageable armful of tulle and silk and lace, ignoring his appraising gaze at her exposed legs and bare feet.

She raised her hand to his face and wagged her finger at him the way she would her most obstinate students at Winnetka Central High School.

"Lieutenant Reeves, you're going to go now, without anything more than a quick goodbye to my parents and the Cabots," she warned.

"All right, ma'am," he replied cautiously.

She almost stopped her train of thought to tell him to stop calling her ma'am, it made her feel a hundred years old, but she decided it wasn't worth it. In five minutes, he'd be gone. A few ma'am's here or there weren't going to make any difference.

She took a deep breath. "I promise you that if you tell anyone here in Winnetka the truth about Parker Cabot IV, so help me I'll follow you to whatever hellhole you and Parker call home and I'll take both of your bodies apart bone by bone by bone.''

His eyes widened and she was sure she had accomplished three very important things.

One, she had impressed upon him the importance of zipping his lip.

Two, she had eliminated any pity he felt for her.

And lastly, unintentionally, she had likely shocked him out of ever calling her ma'am again.

KYLE RESOLVED never to come stateside again. Especially in dress uniform and carrying break-up letters.

Yanking at his tie and struggling with the top button of his uncomfortable shirt, Kyle followed hot on Kate's trail. Her dress billowed behind her, gathering dewdrops and grass clippings into its frothy hem.

She stepped straight through the spray of water from the Cabots' water sprinkler and took the steps to the Lodge front porch two at a time. He raised his hand against the water as he passed the sprinkler.

''Wait a minute! What do you want me to tell those people in there? You know—your parents and Parker's parents and that lady with the pins in her mouth. What am I going to say to them?''

Kate paused at the front door of the Lodge house. ''I think you've said quite enough,'' she said crisply. ''You said you were a friend of Parker's and that he's not coming back. If you feel the need to chat, simply tell them that anything else is…classified. I'll take care of the rest. Call a cab and get out of here. Good day, Lieutenant.''

Kate flung open the front door. Her head throbbed. There were pins sticking into her back. Her stomach growled.

She had just been dumped.

And though she sympathized with Parker, would always regard him affectionately as a brother and was frankly a little relieved that she wasn't going to be his bride, she was just the teensiest bit—make that a lot—furious with him for leaving her with the responsibility of bursting the bubble on the fairy tale believed by all of Winnetka.

"Are you going to show them the letter?" Kyle asked from the doorway. He had followed her into the house.

"I hadn't thought that far in advance," she answered, confronted by the picture displayed on the hall console next to the vase of hyacinths. The fairy-tale hero and his princess.

"That's Parker and you, right?"

She nodded. "Our high school prom."

"I don't think powder blue is Parker's color."

"You're trying to be nice, but I'll tell you the truth. Powder blue is Parker's color. So is every other color in the rainbow. He's...well, he's not really handsome. But he's a golden boy—he's always had an air about him that makes people love him. Maybe it's because he was born so late to the Cabots—they had given up ever having children and then he came to them. Like a miracle. A great, shining miracle.''

"You shine just as brightly," he murmured.

"Have you always been a sweet-talker?"

"Only when I need to be," he replied with the smug assurance of a man who seldom needed sweet-talk in order to get what he wanted.

"Well, you can stop now," she said tartly. "Go back to Parker and tell him that I won't let him— make that, his parents—down.''

She swept past him up the steps, tugging at the zipper of her dress. When the first pin pulled free, she grimaced and thought of the long hours Mrs. Maguire had put into the gown.

Then, suddenly, Kate realized it didn't matter anymore. She was never going to wear it and no Lodge cousin would want to wear a dress with such bad luck associated with it.

She was free—could rip the dress from its collar to its train without guilt. It might even feel good, beyond the mere relief of the pain caused by the tiny pins crisscrossing its back. She yanked the zipper apart, feeling the dress unlock its pincerlike grip on her back just as she reached the top of the stairs.

"Kate."

A ma'am or another reference to her ladylike qualities wouldn't have given her pause.

But the name did it.

She closed her eyes against the pleasure of hearing her name on his lips.

Then she got a hold of herself.

In her haste to get out of the dress and reach the sanctuary of her room, she had forgotten he was still standing at the bottom of the stairs.

Putting her hands up to her breasts to hold the disintegrating dress in place, she reluctantly turned and acknowledged him with the barest nod.

He caught up with her, pausing at the step two short of the second floor. His steel blue eyes sought hers.

She looked away. Lord save her from a charming and handsome man. She'd had quite enough of his kind for one day!

"Are you all right?" he asked, and she knew his question was his final offer.

But Kate was firmly in control of herself, having only indulged for only the briefest moment in wild speculation and delicious daydreams.

"I'm fine, thank you very much. I'm not in a state of shock, if that's what you think. And I'm not about to dissolve into a puddle of tears—it's not my way. Besides, I think deep down I saw this coming."

She tugged at the dress to hold it in place. The dress, weighted down with its voluminous folds, tugged back.

"How are you going to break this to them?" He gestured toward the Cabot house. "They're not as ready for this as you were."

"You surprise me," she said sharply. "I would have thought you were a man who knew when to stay out of other people's business."

"I am that kind of man."

"Then butt out."

She yanked at the dress and heard too late the plaintive, tearing sound. She sprinted for her bedroom at the end of the hall.

Her dress didn't go with her.

Striding away from him wearing nothing more than a flimsy bra and pantie set wasn't very dignified, but Kate held her head as regally as she knew how.

She looked back only once, and then only after she had reached the safety of her bedroom door. He stood on the stairs, her dress puddling around his legs. She knew she would never see him again in her life, and that was the only fact that could make the moment not unendurably embarrassing.

And because she was never going to see him again, something very un-Kate-like happened.

She faced him fully, displaying herself in a way she had never done with a man. He was gifted with a sight of her that only happened once a year in the doctor's office—and then only with a paper gown.

She wanted him to look at her, to see her as a woman.

He was a sophisticated man, of that she had no doubt. He was also a very experienced man—he had had his share of women. Kate could tell by the easy way he had appraised her when she first came down the stairs. And Kate knew she couldn't measure up to the kind of women he most likely bedded. Younger women, eager women, women with more curves and less of a smart mouth than her own. He wasn't going to fall all over himself with passion at the sight of Kate Lodge in her undies.

Maybe later, she would blame it on being a thirty-year-old spinster. She might meet another man with whom she could share her body and her soul and then again, maybe she would never meet such a man. This might be her last chance at...well, at something Kate couldn't quite name.

And so she stood, for no more than a half a minute. Someone who didn't know her well might say she had just gotten flustered, in the way a deer on the highway gets caught by the blazing headlights of an oncoming car. Someone might say her brain was in chaos because of the shock of Parker's rejection. Someone might even say that it was high blood sugar or low blood sugar or no blood sugar at all.

But she knew better.

And she knew that Kyle knew better.

He did what a gentleman should do. He looked at her appreciatively, as if he were awestruck by her beauty—as if he wanted her badly, but was holding himself in check. As if only the most highly developed self-restraint stopped the lieutenant from striding across the hallway and taking her.

And that look on his face, even if it was the work of being a gentleman, could last her until the rest of her life. If it had to.

"Call a cab, Lieutenant Reeves," she said quietly, and closed the door behind her.

KYLE LET OUT a deep, hot breath of air that he hadn't even known he'd been holding. The house was quiet, except for the ticking of the grandfather clock in the front foyer. Within the prism of light cast by an overhead skylight, dust swirled like flakes in a snow globe. The upstairs smelled even more feminine than the rest of the Lodge house—more like roses than vanilla, like sandalwood instead of freshly baked bread.

He stared at the heavy oak door at the end of the hallway, wondering if she were going to come out again.

From his first experiences as a Kentucky youth, he had instinctively known how to read a woman as easily as he would a map. But Kate was such a mass of contradictions that he felt as though he had been spun around a hundred times and left in the wilderness without a compass.

Back there on the Cabots' porch, she had been a delicate flower of a woman, barely able to stand the torment of Parker's rejection. All the time she was just luring him into revealing things about his buddy that he would have ordinarily kept to himself.

And once she had extracted his secrets, had heard every terrible truth without flinching, she dismissed him as if he were a servant.

And Kyle had never been dismissed by a woman.

There on the porch, he was ready to declare that she was trouble—too headstrong and smart-mouthed for his taste in women. He was ready to call that cab and get out. He was nearly ready to commend

Parker on not marrying her—though he would still
tear him apart for his method of breaking the news
and the deception he had wrought on Kate and Kyle
both. He was ready to leave the Cabots and the
Lodges and the woman with the pins in her mouth
to find out about Parker on their own, as Kate saw
fit to break the news.

But the episode at the doorway to her bedroom
changed everything.

Part invitation, part dismissal. Looking a little like
a lost child, still displaying herself like a proud
woman. An intelligent crackle in her eyes, paired
with the utter bafflement of a woman who didn't
know the first thing about pleasuring a man.

Daring him to look, and slamming the door on
him when he did.

She wasn't his idea of bed mate—too tall, too
boyishly skinny, not enough curves and way too
many sharp angles for Kyle.

Still, he smiled at the memory of her as he folded
her torn-up wedding gown and deposited it on a
bench at the bottom of the stairs.

He knew something about Kate that he would bet
his cardamom and tea plantation, on the Sri Lankan
foothills, no one else in Winnetka knew.

Miss Kate Lodge indulged in the kind of underwear that was available only by catalog. And today
she wore green—palest green, a color he would
never have thought of as erotic.

He would have thought she'd be more the type to
wear wool. Boiled wool.

She had a heart of sensuality, but it was hidden as surely as her underwear.

He opened the French door to the living room and looked around for the phone. A quick glance at his watch told him he had an hour yet to meet that naval C-130 flying nonstop to Colombo. He had a spot on that plane.

"I've called the cab company," said Mr. Lodge, who came into the living room from the kitchen. He had two glasses of ice tea on a silver tray. "Taxi should be here in ten minutes. Let's just wait for it on the porch."

Kyle took the tray from him and followed him through the front door. They sat on side by side rocking chairs. Kyle waited for Mr. Lodge to ask him something, something about Parker.

Like: Where is he? When is he coming back? Is he all right?

Kyle wondered if he'd have the sense to lie in a convincing way.

If it were up to him, he'd tell the truth. The whole unvarnished truth. But Kate had asked him to be silent, and he seldom declined the direct requests of a lady.

There were no questions. Mr. Lodge merely rocked back and forth and drank his tea. Silent, so silent that the *swish* of the lawn sprinkler across the street had all the impact of a freight train rushing past.

If Kyle had been on assignment, he wouldn't have trusted this moment of waiting. He would have sensed something was not quite right. But he wasn't on assignment—he was among civilians, trustworthy ones at that.

So he sat back in his rocking chair, sipped his ice tea and appreciated the fact that he didn't have to lie about Parker anymore.

He thought about the punch in the jaw he'd give Parker. Should he use a strong right hook or a left jab? Should he tell him why he was punching him beforehand or should he just punch him and take the consequences? Should he tell Parker his ex-fiancée was devastated or should he tell Parker she was already lining up replacement suitors?

There was a lot to think about.

Chapter Four

"Don't worry, son, that cab's just running a little late," Mr. Lodge said laconically, putting his drained glass on the porch floor by his chair leg. "It'll come."

Kyle tugged at the cuff of his uniform and looked discreetly at his watch. Already thirty past the hour. If the cab came now, he'd still have a shot at making it to the airport. But even an extra ten minutes would put him completely off schedule.

He thought of the pilot, who'd gotten him a berth on the plane because he owed Kyle big-time for saving his brother's life in a firefight in Nicaragua. Kyle wondered how long the pilot could hold the plane on the Glenview Naval Air Base runway.

"What time did you say you called them?"

"Ten-twenty."

Kyle swallowed hard. "Sir, I might be wrong, but I thought you said you called them at ten-fifteen."

"Oh, no, I couldn't possibly have said ten-fifteen," Mr. Lodge said, shaking his head vigorously. "I called at ten-twenty. They'll be here, young man."

"But…"

Mr. Lodge raised his hand to silence Kyle's objections. "I personally know the gentleman who runs the company. Paul Nilson. Absolutely reliable. Very dependable. We'll see his cab turning the corner right there in just a moment, I'm sure. Looky there now."

Mr. Lodge gestured vaguely in the direction of some children racing through a sprinkler. They screamed and giggled and tugged their wet bathing suits into place.

No yellow cab turned the corner.

Kyle forced his breath to still and his heartbeat to slow. He had waited for rescue before and that cab was surely rescue. Every bit as much as an Apache helicopter or a pack of Navy SEALs coming to pull his men out after a job well-done.

He squirmed a bit, remembering a time when he had waited in a Southeast Asian jungle for a helicopter pickup that never came. When he had given up hope, he had led his men on a two-week march to safety. Hadn't lost a man.

But what would he do if the taxi didn't turn that corner? Would it be just as arduous for him to return to the safety of Sri Lanka from Winnetka? Surely not.

But if he didn't get out of Winnetka soon, he was in trouble. Lots of trouble. There'd be a family.

Make that two families. With questions about their little Parker.

And there'd be trouble with a woman. A skinny, freckle-faced redhead with a smart mouth, not enough curves and a too-direct way of looking at a man. A good woman. A beautiful woman, although Kyle wondered at how he had ever come to that conclusion.

She was a Sunday school teacher kind of woman, even if she did sport the intimates of a faster type. The kind of woman who deserved a halo on her head—not his idea of fun at all.

She wouldn't be happy if she came downstairs and found him here on the porch with her father.

"What time did you say you called that cab?" he asked again.

Mr. Lodge closed his eyes as if he were settling in for a long, well-deserved morning nap. "Ten twenty-five," he said. "I'm sure I called the cab company at ten twenty-five."

KYLE KNOCKED ONCE, softly, in case she were sobbing. Come to think of it, sobbing wasn't something she'd do, he decided. Even in the privacy of her own room. Self-reproach, perhaps.

Indignation, certainly.

Embarrassment, no doubt.

But all met with a steady gaze and a head-on determination to make it through another day.

In spite of himself, he admired her. Although it was an admiration mixed with pity. Pity that righteous spinsterhood was now her lot, that Parker had been her miserable excuse of a fiancé, that she'd have nothing more than living in her parents' home for the rest of her life. In a small town in the middle of corn. Lots of corn.

Kyle shuddered. Sounded worse than the brig.

"Who is it?"

The voice growling on the other side of the door was in no mood for him. Or his admiration. Or his pity. His grudging goodwill evaporated. With it, his reflexive courtliness with women.

"It's me. Lieutenant Reeves. If you want me out of here so damn bad, then you've got yourself a problem."

She opened the door, and it was as he registered his disappointment that he realized he had hoped she'd still be in her undies. Instead, she was dressed for a five-mile run or some heavy work in the garden. Her shorts were gray and baggy and topped by a Northwestern University Wildcats T-shirt. Her hair was pulled back in a severe ponytail that accentuated her sharp cheekbones.

Her shoulders were reared back for trouble.

She put one hand on her hip, but kept her other hand firmly on the doorknob.

He was most emphatically not invited in.

"What's the problem?"

"The cab's late. I've got a cargo plane I can hitch a ride on, but if I don't make that plane, I'm stuck here 'til tomorrow. There isn't a commercial flight to Colombo on any airline today."

"You have to call Paul Nilson. He owns the cab company. Ask him to come pick you up."

She had that tone of voice a teacher has with the most dim-witted of her students.

"Your father already did that," Kyle said, hanging on to his patience by reminding himself that she had just been unceremoniously dumped by her fiancé. And she might be in shock. Maybe she was a nice person on an ordinary day.

"When?" she demanded.

"When what?"

"When did he call the cab?"

"Ten, fifteen, twenty minutes ago. Oh, I don't know. I've been waiting quite a while."

"You look like the kind of man who gets what he wants when he wants it," she said.

"I am," he conceded.

"Learn some patience. Go downstairs, sit and wait quietly."

He shoved his boot in the path of the slamming door. Enough treating her like a dainty little lady.

"Call the cab again," he ordered. "If you want me on that plane out of here, lady, you'd better call that cab yourself."

Her eyes flashed like burning opals and for the first time in his adult life, Kyle wasn't sure whether his orders would be obeyed. He clenched his jaw. He wondered again how long the pilot of that cargo jet would wait for him. He wondered if she was always this stubborn. He wondered if she were still wearing the pale green underwear.

And then suddenly there was surrender. She opened the door.

"Fine," she said, giving in only as little as absolutely necessary. "Sit there."

She pointed to a chintz-covered armchair that was the perfect size for a chihuahua but which was certain to collapse under his muscular frame. He sat tentatively, balancing most of his weight on his strong, rock-hard thighs.

He looked about the feminine lair. A pale blue quilt covered the double bed, a pine armoire dominated one corner of the room and sheer lace panels diffused the leaf-dappled sunlight. Kate sat at a delicate bamboo desk, talking softly into the phone. She abruptly hung up and looked over at him with a prim, tight-lipped expression.

"Paul Nilson is running vacation Bible school this morning," she announced.

"So?"

"So that means the Winnetka Cab Company is closed for the day," Kate explained, looking as if she were about to add "you moron." Instead, she explained, "He likes to take a nap in the afternoon if he's worked in the morning. My dad must have misunderstood." She swiped a handful of keys and grabbed her purse from the bed.

"It's thirty minutes to the airport," she said.

Kyle swore. She looked at him as if the word had never been spoken within Winnetka's city limits and carried a fifty-dollar fine.

"We'll never make it in time," Kyle explained.

"That plane was scheduled to take off in just a few minutes. I pulled some favors but that pilot's not going to wait much longer."

"You've never seen me drive."

Actually, Kyle thought as he followed her down the stairs and through the back of the house, he would guess her to be the little-old-lady style of driver. Cautious. A bit hesitant. Coming to a full and complete stop at every corner. Always following the speed limit, maybe even five miles an hour slower. Taking yellow at its word, and waiting for the next green before turning left.

There was no way she'd make it to that airport in time for him to get that plane, but Kyle resigned himself to this exercise in futility. The leisurely ride would give him time to think how to get out of Winnetka.

Yanking open the garage door with one determined pull, Kate would have agreed with him that she was that kind of driver, would have confessed to traffic caution with a certain amount of pride—she had two safety certificates in her wallet.

After all, better safe than sorry.

But she was sorrier still that Lieutenant Reeves was in Winnetka, sorry enough that she peeled out of the garage while Kyle was struggling to close his door, pausing only to slam her hand squarely on the horn to warn children to stay clear of the driveway.

Then, feeling very sorry, she tugged at her own seat belt and slammed her foot on the accelerator.

The squeal could be heard in the next town.

She barely registered the shocked crowd pouring out of the Cabots' front door, yelling and pointing at her from the porch.

Given the time and leisure, Kate would have been sorrier still that she had finally given Winnetka something to talk about and she wasn't even around to savor it.

SITTING on the still-warm hood of her car, Kate leaned back to watch the C-130 transport plane pass over the frontage road. A graceful plane, it rose with deceptive speed and a thunderous roar casting an enormous shadow as it passed before the sun, heading west. The plane left behind a dark, billowing cloud of dust and exhaust and quivering heat.

Kate watched until the plane disappeared on the horizon. Then she reached out to touch the wire fence that ran the perimeter of the air base. Kyle had leapt the fence, racing for the plane in the final desperate moments. She wondered how long it would be before he noticed that, in his haste, he had left his duffel in her back seat.

So how would she get it to him? And how was she going to get the car out of the grassy ditch?

She looked back at the deep, muddy tracks her car had left from the edge of the road down the grassy slope and across the lightly graveled shoulder. She had more immediate problems than how to get Lieutenant Reeves his duffel bag.

She sighed, got up and tried to wipe off a splatter of mud on her leg only to make it worse.

Maybe the strenuous physical effort of pushing her car up to the frontage road would be good for her. If nothing else, it might eliminate thoughts she'd had—so funny, really—to grab Lieutenant Reeves by the sleeve and beg him to let her come with him. To whatever world there was on the other side of a fifteen-hour airplane ride.

But she was dependable, responsible, sensible Kate. She would do the right thing. After all, others relied on her.

She got in her car and tried to back out onto the frontage road, but the wheels spun uselessly in the mud. Muttering a word she hadn't known was in her vocabulary—the very same word Kyle had used in her bedroom—she popped the clutch into Neutral and walked around to the front of the car.

Taking a deep gulp of air, she leaned forward and put her shoulder on the grille and her feet as firmly in the muck as she could.

She pushed. She grunted. She shoved. She rubbed her hands together, took another deep breath and tried again. Her legs fought for purchase on the wet, grassy slope. She stood up, shaking her head at her skinny, mud-splattered arms. She crouched again, put her body into it and pushed.

And pushed and pushed.

She lost her footing and fell face first into the mud. Her eyes stung. Her mouth tasted the grit of mud and the green of grass.

And then she started to cry. Not dainty little tears falling down her cheeks. Loud, heaving sobs with huge gasps for air when her lungs burned empty. Her cheeks were soaked with tears and mud, her shoulders convulsed underneath her mud-splattered T-shirt.

Giving up on the car, she sat up and howled, letting all her grief out.

After all, she was alone. No one was depending on her right now. She could let it come.

And it came. All of it. The pain and the hurt and the frustrations and the fears for the future. All of it, in one big cry.

She didn't see him walking from out of the cloud left in the plane's wake, or climbing the fence in one easy hand-over-hand. Didn't see him standing over her, a mixture of resignation and unexpected softness on his face.

She felt his hands first, as he crouched to wrap her shoulders in a strong, compassionate grip. She gulped, and leaned her head back to lay upon his chest, bumpy from the bar of medals he had to wear. Her breath came ragged as she tried to pull herself together. But he didn't seem to expect that of her. Didn't seem to demand her strength or composure or her good nature. No, he brought her into his arms, fully into his embrace. And allowed her to cry, as a woman who'd had a bad, bad day.

"Cry it out," he soothed, although she was taking that advice long before he gave it.

When she was finished, she let out a big sigh and pulled her head out from his chest. She looked up at him with wide, reddened eyes.

HE WANTED TO kiss her.

Kyle wasn't the kind of man who just kissed a woman. Oh, he liked women. Liked kissing. No doubts about either. He liked everything about making love to a woman—the kissing and caressing and the final moment of ecstasy. All of it was good.

But kissing by itself, not as part of a seduction, wasn't anything he had ever given a thought to. Just a kiss was like eating one bite of a meal and Kyle was the kind of man who satisfied his appetites.

Until this moment.

He knew it wouldn't go any further. She didn't look like the kind of woman who would make love on a mud-splattered ditch on a road at the backside of an airport. No, Kate looked like the kind of woman who only made love on a bed covered by crisply ironed sheets and at least one carat on her left hand.

So if he kissed her, it would be just that.

A kiss.

No more.

He had never kissed a woman with those constraints before.

With no guarantees that Kate wouldn't haul off and slug him, he tipped her chin up with his cupped hand and bent down to taste her full, pink lips. A man knowledgeable of sophisticated pleasures, he started to close his eyes just as his demanding flesh met her softness.

And he noticed her wide, unblinking stare.

He jerked back.

"Don't kiss me if it's pity," she said defiantly.

She had laid down a challenge and he'd be damned if he would back down. He'd kiss her the way he kissed any woman. Taking his pleasure and giving as much as he got.

"It's not pity," he growled.

He scooped her up in his arms, his dress uniform be damned, and kissed her. Really kissed her. The way a woman should be kissed.

She tasted of dirt and peppermint and smelled of the soft vanilla of her sex. Her lips opened to his demanding tongue and he explored her flesh and brought her to a shivering plateau of pleasure.

She squirmed as if to escape from him and then just as suddenly moaned for more—and he knew that she had never been kissed like this before.

He abruptly released her, honoring his own code of gentlemanliness that included not taking advantage of the innocents, whether technically virgins or not.

She stared up at him, kneeling in the mud, her eyes wondrously blue-green like the South China Sea on a summer morning. He could push her for more, but he wouldn't.

"I missed my plane," he said, standing. "I ran as fast as I could and I still missed it. I checked and there's a commercial flight out of O'Hare Airport tomorrow morning. I'll get that one."

"You darn well better."

If he didn't have a firm rule on never speaking sharply to a lady, he would have been tempted.

She was subdued as she sat in the driver's seat and switched on the ignition, popping the clutch into Reverse.

He pushed. He shoved. He grimaced. He groaned.

And with a triumphant roar, launched the car up onto the frontage road.

He reached into the back seat for his duffel.

"All right, Kate, this is it. Goodbye," he said. "I'll walk to O'Hare from here. Have a nice life. Awfully sorry about Parker."

She looked at him and her lip curled ever so slightly into a resigned smile. "Get in the car," she ordered. "They're not letting you into the airport looking like that."

He looked down at his uniform. Soaked in mud. The sleeve of his jacket ripped from its shoulder. His shirt missing a few buttons.

He shook his head, defeated. "I guess you're right."

He shoved the duffel back into the car and got into the front seat.

"Just don't say a word to anybody," she warned without looking at him. "And remember—it's just for tonight. I want you on that plane tomorrow morning."

"Don't worry, I'll be on that plane."

"And not a word," Kate repeated. "You keep your mouth shut, understand?"

He started to tell her that he didn't want to be here in the first place, that he hated being anywhere except on assignment, that he nearly burst his lungs trying to run after that transport plane. Nothing would give him more pleasure than to get on a plane and get out. And he had no burning desire to talk to any of the fine people of Winnetka.

Come to think of it, he never liked good women—prim, prissy women like her—anyway. He liked curves and good times and blond hair, definitely blondes.

But, as he touched his lips, those words died unsaid, and he realized that their kiss had not just been a kiss.

Chapter Five

"So when are you going to tell them?" Kyle asked as they approached the first stoplight on Willow Road heading back to Winnetka from Glenview.

Kate startled. She had been using deep-breathing exercises—the ones she had read about in the magazine at the dentist's office last week—to calm herself. She checked the rearview mirror.

Her face was the color of a ripening peach, with a big slash of mud across her cheeks. Her eyes had a restless quality. Her mouth felt bruised and tingly. Were her lips swollen or had they always had that bee-stung quality?

Anybody who saw her would know she'd been in some trouble. But could they tell what kind of trouble—the kissing kind?

Take a deep breath, she cautioned herself, putting the mirror back into place and tapping the accelerator. *Hold the air for the count of four, and breathe out while thinking of a cool, restful place.*

The refrigerator, for instance.

She glanced at Kyle, who had taken his handkerchief and was wiping the worst of the mud from his jaw. But he missed some on his cheek. Kate nearly reached out to take the cloth from his hand.

It wouldn't do to come back home and have everyone see their matching mud streaks.

But it'd be worse to reach out and touch him again. She might never stop. What kind of sickness had overcome her that her hormones were in total overdrive?

She wrapped her fingers around the steering wheel more tightly.

She had, until he had spoken, forgotten that her primary problem wasn't recovering from a kiss. A kiss so shocking and passionate that it had blotted out everything else and made her hunger for more.

But now she could focus and she knew she had problems that went beyond the merely physical. She was twenty minutes outside of Winnetka and she had trouble in the car with her. And Parker's reputation, the Cabots' honor and her own family's life-long friendship at stake.

"Tell them what?" she asked, eyes narrowing. "What part are you talking about?"

"The part where he's not coming back for good. All I said was that he wasn't coming back today."

"Oh, that. I guess I have to do something before tomorrow."

"Why before tomorrow?"

"Tomorrow's Fourth of July."

"Oh, yeah, right, Fourth of July," Kyle said.

"Best to get bad news out of the way before the fireworks."

"It's only because he's the grand marshal."

"He's what?"

"The grand marshal," Kate repeated with just a smidgen of bitterness, knowing what she knew now about Winnetka's favorite hero. "He was supposed to lead the Fourth of July parade. Actually he would be right behind the Boy Scouts carrying the color guard, and he was going to give a speech on the village green."

"No wonder he doesn't want to come home," Kyle murmured.

Kate shot him a venomous look. "It's not funny. A whole town was counting on him. Posters are up in every store window in town and the park district sent home a flyer with all the kids in day camp. The *Winnetka Talk* ran an article about him just last week. The speech was going to be pretty good—it was called 'Heroism in Southeast Asia.'"

"'Heroism in Southeast Asia'?" Kyle sputtered. "Parker wouldn't know anything about the topic."

"Oh, he knows quite a bit," Kate said coolly. She leveled a fixed gaze on him. "Southeast Asia is where he saved your life, remember?"

Kyle slammed his open palm on the dashboard.

He stared at the unforgiving horizon of Northern Illinois farmland. Corn was just coming up, its rows spinning by like spokes on a wheel.

Kate slowed to a stop at the light on Pfingsten Road. She wondered what could be done about the parade. So many people had been looking forward to it....

"Light's changed," Kyle said blandly. "It's green. You can go."

"Oh, sorry."

"Who's going to be in that parade?"

"I suppose they'll get the fire marshal. Or the sheriff. My father'll take the mayor aside and have him decide—he's pretty discreet."

"What are you going to tell the Cabots and your parents when you tell them the whole story?"

Kate took a deep, fortifying breath. "I'm going to say that Kyle has been asked to be part of an elite rapid reaction unit and cannot return home," she said. "And he feels it's best to release me from our promise to marry because I would have to wait so long for him and in such uncertainty." She took in his openmouthed wonder. "And you're not going to say or do anything in the next twenty-four hours to contradict me!"

Kyle laughed without humor. "Lady, I don't care what you tell the home crowd," he said. "All I care about is..."

"Is what?"

He looked at her, and she self-consciously raked the back of her hand across her cheeks. Wondering how much mud she still had on her.

"Nothing," he said, staring pointedly out the window. "I don't care about nuthin'."

THE SHERIFF'S SQUAD CAR and Mayor Cruikshank's black Pontiac sedan were parked along the curb at the Lodge house. When Kate pulled her car into the driveway, the two officials rose from their chairs on her porch. The screen door swung open—Mr. Lodge, Mr. Cabot and several of the neighbors followed the official delegation out to the driveway.

Kate got out of the car, saw the expressions of shock and she wondered for one wild moment if everyone in Winnetka knew that she had just been kissed within an inch of her life.

She took in their dumbfounded gazes and looked at Kyle and herself through their eyes.

Kyle's face might be rugged and relatively clean and bearing a good-natured grin, but his uniform was torn and muddy.

And as for herself... She winced as she looked down at the damage.

"The car got stuck," she explained.

But that explanation left out anything that would have made any sense. Mayor Cruikshank's eyebrows drew together. The sheriff worried his badge. Mrs. Cabot peered uncertainly. Her own father took off his glasses and rubbed them with the hem of his cardigan—a sure sign he was not following her.

She tried again.

"At the airport," she said carefully. "I was taking him to the airport."

Five simultaneous nods, as if the town's leading citizens had turned into cows chewing their cud. But the rest of the gathering on the driveway remained mute and motionless.

She guiltily touched her mouth. She felt more exposed than if she had been stark naked on the corner of Elm and Lincoln Avenues, the only Winnetka street corner busy enough to warrant a light.

"The car got stuck in the mud at the airport," she said all at once, her explanation beginning to take on the singsong quality of a Dr. Seuss rhyme.

"Sorry to hear that," said Mr. Cruikshank.

And then he clapped his hands together. He was a man who was used to having to move the agenda along at town hall meetings and this was definitely an agenda-moving moment.

"We have come to a consensus on what to do about the parade," he said loudly, directing his words to the entire gathering. "Now, I don't mean to pry into your personal affairs, Kate, but I understand Parker will not be getting back home in time for tomorrow's ten o'clock start of the parade?"

Kate opened her mouth and then closed it. She hadn't really wanted to make any announcements in the middle of her driveway with mud caked all over her body and Kyle Reeves standing on the other side of her car. She had envisioned something with a little more dignity. Maybe in the living room over some sherry with the two families gathered around and her words carefully rehearsed. This was the sort of thing she usually wrote out index cards for. But she did the best she could.

"He won't...be back...for the parade."

Accustomed to steering Winnetka through all manner of municipal turmoil, Mr. Cruikshank registered his disappointment with only a small cough. He immediately turned his gaze on Kyle.

"Then we humbly request that you, young man, as friend of our town's greatest hero, take his place at the head of the parade," he said with great ceremony. He leaned forward and added conspiratorially, "You'll get to ride on the back seat of my personal vehicle—a 1967 pink Cadillac. Mint condition. I'll be taking the cover off it and waxing it up tonight."

Having offered up the greatest enticement imaginable, Mr. Cruikshank rested his weight on his heels and waited for Kyle's reply.

Kyle looked over the top of the car at Kate. She pursed her lips together to stop herself from shouting "No!" but allowed herself an urgent shiver of her head to indicate her absolute, no-holds-barred, non-negotiable opposition to him leading the parade.

All while trying to appear to be sweetly encouraging him, for the purposes of the crowd staring poker-faced at the couple.

Kyle looked at her. She knew he knew.

"Hmm," he replied to the mayor. "I couldn't possibly take Parker's place," he said and then a double-dare-you smile played across his face. "But I am honored by the invitation...."

She was just about to throw herself on the driveway and beg him to get on that next plane and get out of here!

He lifted the ripped, muddy shoulder seams of his jacket and shook his head ruefully at the mayor. "I would be most honored, but I only have one dress uniform and it is now ruined.''

Kate let go of a breath she hadn't known she had been holding and uttered a prayer of thanksgiving that had begun as a plea for mercy.

He wouldn't do the parade.

He'd quietly get on tomorrow's flight.

She'd take her family and the Cabots aside, breaking the news of Parker's letter with that long-sought dignity. Reassuring the Cabots that it was her pleasure and duty to help them through the coming years in whatever way a daughter-in-law would have. Then she'd let her mother handle the phone calls to the neighbors—from there the news would travel fast.

By Sunday evening, she'd be a confirmed spinster. She wasn't sure how her life would be much different because of a change in marital status from engaged at a distance to single.

Mr. Cruikshank steepled his fingers together. ''I don't think that your uniform presents an insurmountable problem,'' he opined.

The balloon popped on Kate's soothing thoughts.

''It doesn't?'' Kyle asked warily.

''It doesn't?'' Kate chorused.

''Oh, no, of course not. Mrs. Maguire can fix whatever little rips there are in the lieutenant's uniform and Mr. Zengeler, the owner of our town's dry-cleaning establishment, can have it spiffed up good as new by morning.''

"I HATE PARADES, Kate."

Kate kept her eyes trained on the row of purple irises she had cultivated to perfection through the warmer-than-usual spring and early summer.

They had showered and dressed—separately, of course. Kyle's uniform had been carried off by Mrs. Maguire. And now in the garden they awaited the call to dinner at the Lodge household for the two families.

Kyle would be asked to sit at the head of the table.

Kate would resist the urge to strangle him.

"You could have said no," she accused. "A flat-out no."

She turned to look at him as he adjusted the chaise longue so that he was nearly supine. He wore a faded pair of jeans that accentuated his rock-hard thighs and his tight groin.

She looked away. Kate wasn't used to noticing carnal features on a man, and she wasn't, just wasn't, going to start now.

"What was I supposed to do after they brought in the lady with the pins in her mouth and the man from the dry cleaner's?"

"No! You were supposed to say no. It's a very simple word. What part don't you understand? The *n* or the *o?*"

"I couldn't say no," he said, closing his eyes against the late sun. "I couldn't say no because you were so opposed to me saying yes. I said yes just to spite you, Kate, and I can't figure out for the life of me why you should matter enough to me that I'd endure a parade and give a speech just to get your goat.''

After an initial moment of righteous indignation, Kate felt oddly pleased to hear this confession. And she was more quick with forgiveness than any minister would have been. After all, she taught school. Hadn't she noticed a hundred times how when a boy liked a girl, he often acted exactly contrary to the dictates of gentlemanly courtship?

He liked her. Or, at the very least, was affected by her.

What an odd and interesting thought. It pleased her.

She looked at him, really looked at him because his eyes were closed and he wouldn't know of her interest.

He was handsome in an offhand, irritating kind of way that perfect men are. Sandy hair, ruddy complexion, strong jaw, perfectly sculpted muscles. Saved from being too handsome only by a tiny white scar directly under his right eye.

But handsomeness wasn't what made him so attractive—it was maleness. His utter and complete comfort with being a man. Being a strong, sometimes rough, sometimes slyly courtly man. Now sprawled on her parents' chaise like a sated tiger.

As a newly created spinster, she was all too aware of the yawning differences between the sexes and she knew that her contact with men—virile, handsome men—was going to fade through the coming years as surely as her irises would over the course of the summer.

Still, this was a man she needed to watch for less than sensual reasons. Every minute between now and when he left town she had to watch him—and make sure he said nothing to compromise Parker's reputation and the reputation of the Cabot family. Or her own family's reputation. Come to think of it, all of Winnetka's reputation was riding on this.

And to secure that reputation, Kyle Reeves had to leave town but fast! If he breathed so much as a word of the truth...

No more mooning over how dreamy he looks! she chastised herself.

Dreamy?

Kate Lodge even thinking the word *dreamy?* She really had lost her mind.

And then she thought she saw the twinkle of blue at his eyelashes. She waved her hand over his face. His face muscles didn't move.

Good. He didn't know she was watching him.

Setting her mouth in a determined grimace, she made a V with her index and middle fingers and made like she was going to poke him in the eyes.

He caught her wrist with a lightning-quick pincer movement.

"You had your eyes open all along!" she accused, squirming out of his grasp.

"You were ogling me."

"I was not!"

"You were, too," he said. He smiled lazily. "Admit it. You were thinking about it."

"It?"

"Sex. You and me."

She crossed her arms in front of her chest. "I was not."

"It's all right," he reassured her, resting his weight on one elbow and provocatively laying his other hand on his thigh. She forced herself to look him square in the face. "I don't mind you thinking about sex, making love, at all."

"I mind very much. I wasn't thinking that way at all."

"Then you're more of a goody two-shoes that I gave you credit for. What were you thinking about?"

"Your speech," she said acidly, pulling a sheaf of index cards from the oversize pocket of her sundress. "Here. Read it and memorize it. If you're fool enough to do a parade and a speech just to spite me, you'll have to have something to say."

He looked at her cards disdainfully.

"I don't take orders from people who don't outrank me or who don't say the magic word."

She stared heavenward. "Please read it. Please memorize it."

"All right," he said, taking the cards. He looked at the first one.

She leaned down to pull some weeds out from the iris bed.

"More than two hundred years ago, our founding

fathers and mothers revolted against the tyranny of a foreign sovereign.''

He paused.

She looked up.

''Kate, this is very boring. I'm going to put these folks to sleep.''

She sighed. Keeping Kyle in line was going to be harder than she had even imagined.

''It might be boring but you're going to...I mean, please, I'd like you to read it. Even if it is boring.''

''And what was Parker going to talk about again?''

''About how he saved your life,'' she said from behind clenched teeth.

''Okay. His speech was going to be a lie. An entertaining speech, but still, a big, fat whopper of a lie,'' Kyle pointed out. He looked down at her carefully crafted outline. Complete with blue highlighted stars at the major points. ''This thing you've written, on the other hand, is the truth. But it's a real snore.''

She stood up, yanking a handful of grass and weeds with her.

''Just go back to where you came from!'' she demanded. ''Go back to where you came from, right after you read this boring speech, and make sure that you have a wonderful life.''

''And just what do you think is back there for me?''

''Adventure. Romance. Experiences. Courage. Excitement. Life. Everything that this small town doesn't have.''

"And all that's back there in Sri Lanka?" he asked, thinking of the heat and the poverty and the dull routines and the drinking buddies. And the loneliness. Yes, the loneliness of a soldier's life.

"All of it's back there," Kate persisted. "The real living is all back there."

"And what's here?"

She threw up her hands in frustration, trailing a shower of green from her fingers. "Responsibility. Safety. Family. Work. Tradition. Boredom."

She sighed heavily, worn out by the weight of her own words.

"Kate, I've been with you most of the day," he said quietly, "and one thing I've not been is bored. Until you made me read this speech."

He held out the index cards to her and silently demanded she take them back. When she reached out, her hand touched his and she felt the shiver of electricity. They both stared at their hands.

She wondered if he would kiss her again.

He seemed to wonder the same thing.

She jerked back, remembering how the kiss had affected her. She had had to turn the shower temperature to nearly ice. The index cards scattered on the lawn between them. "Don't make me feel something for you," she warned. "You're going back to Sri Lanka tomorrow right after you read this speech, even if you have to sleep in the airport until the next plane."

"I didn't ask you to go anywhere with me and I'm not trying to make you feel one way or another," he said mildly. "I only thought we could have some fun. I'm sorry if the sexual invitation offended you. Fun, Kate, that's all I was talking about. Fun."

"Apology accepted," she said curtly, struggling to regain her composure. "But Kyle, you should have known—I am most definitely not the kind of woman who has fun."

She swept away, running toward the house as much to escape her own frustrations as his appraising gaze. It was so unfair that she was always the responsible one.

Why couldn't she be the one with the adventures?

KYLE PICKED UP the index cards.

"More than two hundred years ago, our founding fathers and mothers..." he read.

He turned around to catch a glimpse of her as she slammed the back door of the Lodge house.

"You're absolutely right," he minced, catching her prissy voice just right. "You're most definitely not the kind of woman who has fun."

Chapter Six

"Try to act like we're friends," Kate said, squeezing onto the back of the mayor's prized 1967 pink Cadillac with the help of one of the Boy Scouts.

As she arranged her white linen skirt dotted with blue and red stars, her young escort trotted back to his position on the color guard ahead of them.

The twelve flags—the State of Illinois, the Stars and Stripes, the Betsy Ross, and others—rustled proudly in the light breeze coming off the lake. The morning was clear and sunny—just right for a Fourth of July parade.

"But Kate, I've always been your friend," Kyle roused in mocking protest. "After all, I'm the very best friend of your fiancé, who is unavoidably detained protecting his country from extraordinary dangers in foreign lands."

Kate stared up at the clear blue sky and counted to ten.

"He saved my life, remember?" Kyle asked with a wicked smile.

"Don't remind me. Just wave to the crowd and

keep your mouth shut. Not a word, Kyle, not a single word out of your mouth.''

His grin only widened, revealing perfect straight, white teeth.

"All right," she pleaded. "Please not a word."

"What about the speech?" he asked slyly. "Do I keep my mouth shut during the speech?"

"No. Then you talk. After the speech you shut up again. And I'll drive you to the airport. We should get there with some time to spare."

"For being a friend, you sound awfully glad to be rid of me."

"Two more hours," she warned. "We've got just two more hours. Three, tops. Then we'll never see each other again. And you can send my love to Parker."

The previous evening—through dinner at the Lodges' and dessert served on the wraparound porch of the Cabot home—the elder parents had readily accepted the cover story Kyle told about Parker serving his country.

"I'm sorry, sir. That's classified information," Kyle had repeated at every turn, shooting Kate sly glances that kept her guessing if he might, just might, blow Parker's cover with the next answer.

But he hadn't.

"I honestly don't know the answer to that one, Mr. Cabot. I haven't got the security clearance to be informed in that respect."

"I regret, ma'am, that I can't answer that."

"Sir, I'm sorry, regulations forbid me from revealing what little I know."

Finally, to forestall any further interrogation, he had simply stiffened with a look of wistful regret.

"Just rest assured that Parker is doing an outstanding job in the field," he had said.

Outstanding job in the field, indeed. Parker's most notable contribution to the Special Forces unit had been the introduction of two very popular mixed drinks—the Tatler Sea Breeze and the Watermelon Daiquiri—to the list of offerings at his bar. Still, the two drinks—in fact, Parker himself—had brought great comfort to many a soldier. Although Kyle himself was a beer man, when he drank at all.

"And Parker spoke frequently of his desire to sacrifice his own comfort for the peace and security we enjoy here in Winnetka," Kate had added as she'd handed out dainty cups of tapioca pudding from a tray she'd carried onto the porch from the Cabot kitchen.

Inspiring words, and there'd been a murmur throughout the lawn and steps where friends and neighbors had gathered upon finding out that Parker's best friend was eating dinner with the two families.

One of the neighbor's teenage daughters had sighed and said it was all terribly romantic.

"What about the wedding?" Kate's mom had asked loudly. "Is he going to make it home in time for the wedding?"

''Mom!'' Kate had shushed. ''We'll worry about that later. Let's just get through the parade.''

LET'S JUST GET THROUGH *the parade*, Kate told herself as she inspected Parker's uniform. Mrs. Maguire had stitched it back together perfectly, and Mr. Zengeler had managed to get out all of the mud stains.

With his regal bearing and dress blues, Kyle could have been a model for a recruiting poster. No, not for a recruiting poster—more like for a beefcake calendar.

If only he'd loosen his tie and let her run her hands through his sandy close-cropped hair.

She felt a sudden, red hot blush. Where had these thoughts come from? She had never, ever been the kind of woman with a sexual imagination.

But he had invaded her thoughts, ruined her night, intruded on her dreams. And when she had awoke at four in the morning, she had stared longingly across the bower of oak trees that ran from her window to the window of Parker's bedroom, where Kyle slept. When she and Parker had been kids, they had climbed the bower to each other's rooms—and now she wondered what Kyle would do if she slipped open the casement, pulled herself to the ledge of Parker's window and knocked.

Would he let her in? Of course, because he was that much of a gentleman.

Would he laugh at her? No, because he was that much of a gentleman.

Would he make love to her? Yes, of course, because he wasn't that much of a gentleman.

"Where's the rest of the parade?" Kyle asked, craning his neck around to see the Boy Scouts chasing the Girl Scouts, and the children of the community nursery school being corralled by their teachers. The town's fire engine and ambulance were parked at the curb, glistening from a new wax job.

The showcase of Winnetka's July Fourth celebration—the high school marching band—was gathering on the school's front lawn. Trombones bleating and flutes twittering. The drum majors flirting with the row of clarinets.

"This is pretty much it," Kate said. She gestured across the school's lawn to twenty grim teens in blue blazers and khaki pants. "That's the high school football team."

"What's their problem?"

The mayor directed the players to line up behind the pink Cadillac. The boys, as surly as only teenaged males can be, nodded at Kate and stood in a halfhearted line. Joe, the quarterback, barely managed a shrug and a smile in Kate's direction.

"They were looking forward to Parker coming home," she said. "For the past few years I've been coaching the team because the principal was keeping the job open for Parker. That's in addition to my regular duties teaching English."

"Are you any good at coaching?"

"I don't think a team should be judged merely on

the basis of whether it wins or loses games. It's really more important to raise self-esteem and confidence and a sense of teamwork."

"That bad, huh?"

"Last season we only won one game," she confessed, the memory of each game hurting in its own way. Not for herself, but for the increasingly demoralized boys. "And that victory was only because the other team didn't show up."

"Parker was supposed to change all that by coming home and taking over."

"Yes, he was."

"What does he know about football?"

"He was the star quarterback for three years," she replied. "He took our team to the state championships two years in a row."

She wondered where Winnetka would find a coach. A good coach. One that would get this down-on-themselves group of teens to enjoy the game.

"Well, try to put a smile on your face," Kyle said. "We're supposed to be leading a parade. The Fourth is generally considered a fun holiday."

"I'm just thinking of all the ways this town is going to suffer. It'll be at least another year before we can hire a real coach—and everyone lived through defeats by telling themselves that as soon as Parker got home, it would be different."

"Until you find a replacement, you're staring at another losing season?"

"I think so. And there are other problems. I run the community blood drive every year—and I know the reason we do so well is because we play up how every pint helps a soldier like Parker. My dad still runs his hardware store because we thought Parker could take over when he came home.''

"Parker left a lot for you to take care of.''

"He sure did,'' Kate agreed. "And then, of course, there are our parents, who are ready—really ready—to retire, and all four need a lot of extra help. They've all looked forward to joining the families.''

"And you can't leave. Can't go and find your own adventures.''

Kate grimaced, thinking of her outburst the evening before. "No, I can't leave. They depend on me.''

"Will you really never give yourself to another man?''

She looked sharply at him. "The only available man in town is Mr. Frumble the librarian. He's sixty-three and wears a hairpiece. I might have actually been telling you the truth when I said that I won't have another man ever again.''

And, before he could tease her any further, she turned away to devote her attention to Mayor Cruikshank, who was frantically directing parade marchers into place. But every time he got a group lined up, another group would dissolve into chaos.

"All right, Boy Scouts, let's get a little more even!'' Mr. Cruikshank shouted into a bullhorn. "Is the band ready? Do the Girl Scouts have their banners? Get those drummers off the fire engine!''

Other than Kate and Kyle, nobody paid him the slightest bit of attention.

Mr. Cruikshank tried clapping his hands. He blew a whistle he wore around his neck. He even leaned over the driver's side door of his Cadillac and blew the horn long and loud.

Several of the Boy Scouts were squirting water guns at the girls. The football team had broken rank, the defensive linesmen good-naturedly tackled Joe to the grass over some imagined offense. The bugle division of the band started to play a recently released heavy-metal tune while the flutes countered with a jazzy version of "Twinkle, Twinkle, Little Star."

"Aw, come on, guys," Mr. Cruikshank moaned, shaking his head as he chased after a Boy Scout who had smudged dirty fingerprints on the car.

Kyle stood up.

"Hey, don't put your feet on his upholstery," Kate warned. "Mayor Cruikshank loves this car so much that..."

Ignoring her, Kyle stood on the trunk of the car.

"Listen up, parade marchers!" he shouted, his voice deep and commanding.

Spinning on his heels, Mayor Cruikshank blubbered about shoe marks on his vintage vehicle, but stopped as he noticed that he was the only one making a sound.

There was silence.

Utter silence on the stretch of Elm Street where the parade was forming. The football players on the grass looked up. The flutists paused, their instruments held aloft. The Boy Scouts stared. Kate looked up at the man who had suddenly brought order to the general chaos of the Winnetka-style parade.

It was just a small town.

It was just a small parade.

But Kyle applied as much of his implacable soldier's strength to this as he would to the most dire, life-threatening circumstance. Here was a man who inspired confidence and a loyal following, Kate thought with an oddly proprietary pride.

He'd need all his strength to keep this group in order.

"You have been given a great responsibility," Kyle said loudly. And Kate knew his voice was carrying, because the drummers at the very back of the band had stopped throwing spitballs at each other.

"What's a responsi-si-si?" a nursery school boy asked.

"A promise," Kyle explained. "You have made a promise with this march. You have promised every soldier who has laid down his life, every sailor who has drowned at sea, every fighter pilot who has been shot down—that everything they did, every sacrifice they made—has been worth it. And that you thank them."

Kate stared up at him. He towered over her. His spit-polished shoes were at eye level.

"Kyle, uh, maybe you should sit down," Kate interrupted, thinking of the mayor's car.

But Kyle wasn't finished.

"So when we march today, we're not marching to have fun or show off for our parents or our friends. We're not marching because we have to or because it's a kick. We're marching for the ones who aren't here. The ones who wish they could be with you. The ones who gave everything so that you would be able to march. The heroes who are still out there protecting us from dangers we don't even know about."

"Like Parker!" someone shouted.

Kyle winced and Kate thought he might jump off the car and leave. Leave the whole town to its paganlike worship of the bartender residing in Sri Lanka. But Kyle merely nodded.

"Yes, that's right. Parker. March for Parker," Kyle said. "March for him and the heroes. March for all of them."

The football players on the lawn looked at each other uncertainly. Joe shrugged. Kate recognized the moment of indecision—should they think Kyle was a fool or would they accept his orders? Kate would bet money on a smart comment. And she figured her quarterback for the mouth.

"March for the heroes," Kyle encouraged again.

Joe wiped the dirt from his hand and motioned to his teammates, playing it cool, but still accepting Kyle's authority. Within seconds, the football team had lined up in its assigned slot behind the nursery school. Not as tightly as a trained corps, but better than anything Winnetka had ever seen.

The Boy Scouts, the Girl Scouts, even the nursery school kids and the marching band stood in lines as straight as a field of corn.

"Well, that's dandy work there, Lieutenant," Mayor Cruikshank said, reaching into his pocket for his keys. "It's not like what we would expect with Parker, but you're not bad, young man."

Kyle jumped off the hood. With the sleeve of his suit jacket, Mayor Cruikshank rubbed the few smudges Kyle had left on the trunk. Then he got into the drivers' seat and honked his horn at the color guard to signal the beginning of the parade.

"You've just wasted your best lines," Kate muttered as Kyle sat next to her. She knew she should thank him, but knew she couldn't. Because a thank-you would remind her of the difference between the man Kyle was and the man her fiancé—make that ex-fiancé—truly was. A thank-you would bring tears to her eyes, because this was going to be the best moment for Winnetka, the shining moment before all hell broke loose, the wondrous moment of peace before she had to tell everyone their hero wasn't coming home.

"I might have wasted a few lines here or there," Kyle murmured in her ear. "But I've got a mighty fine speech right here in my breast pocket. 'More than two hundred years ago, our founding fathers and mothers revolted against the tyranny of a foreign sovereign.'"

They lurched forward and the marching band picked up the first bars of "Columbia, the Gem of the Ocean.'' As the notes began to come together into an actual melody, Kate realized she couldn't cage a man like Kyle with a pack of primly written index cards.

He was as powerful in his choice of words as he probably was on the field of battle. A flat-out snoozer of a speech was what she had given him. She regretted that now.

"Give me my speech back," she suggested. "You say what you want to say."

"The truth?" he challenged.

She hesitated. The truth would be devastating.

"Is the truth what you really want to say?" she asked.

"I'm an honest man. I don't mind lying to desks, but lying to civilians is a little different."

"Then I guess you'd better stick with the index cards. Because I'm the one who would have to deal with the consequences of the truth, and I'm a coward."

"You're not a coward, Kate," Kyle said softly, his warm breath at the wispy curls that had escaped the chignon she had twisted at her neck. "You're the bravest woman I know."

She flushed at his compliment, but hid her embarrassment by vigorously waving to the crowd lining the curb. The littlest kids wore paper hats and baseball caps. They waved tiny flags and their grandparents sat in folding chairs on the curb.

At either side of the Cadillac, the clerks from Lakeside Groceries pushed grocery carts filled with candy and threw the treats to the roaring crowd. The whole town was either marching in the parade or supporting it from the sidelines.

Kate smiled and waved to all the people she knew, though her heart was breaking for her town. And for herself.

She looked at the man beside her. He waved and graciously accepted the occasional handshake from someone who ran into the street. She looked at him and knew that Winnetka might recover from losing its faith in its favorite hero, but she would not recover from the knowledge that she would never, ever have this man.

And that she had to do everything in her power to get him out of Winnetka as quickly as possible.

"You are going to read the speech I gave you, aren't you?" she asked him, without breaking her smile to the crowd. "I mean, I know I just said you could say whatever you wanted to, but you could hurt so many people by destroying Parker."

"Don't you feel angry at him for what he did? At least for what he did to you, if not this whole town?"

"Sure," she said. "At least, I'm mad about how he broke up with me and how he deceived his family, my family, an entire town. But I would never destroy other people's feelings just to get back at him. Kyle, please, read the speech the way I gave it to you."

"And what are you going to do for me in return?"

She wasn't sure she had heard him correctly but when their eyes locked, she knew exactly, precisely, what he was saying.

Did he really mean to make such a suggestion of trading...? Or was he just playing with her?

It was offensive and yet oddly pleasurable at the same time. It. Sex.

Her breath caught, and suddenly she wondered if everyone in Winnetka, the entire town, would collectively gasp at the suggestive way he was looking at her. And she at him.

But then she was reminded by the sea of faces at curbside, the rippling flags, the shrieks of delight, and knew that no one in Winnetka knew this secret exchange.

"I'll promise you whatever you want. Is that the answer you were looking for?" she asked, trying to sound as playful as he did, but knowing she fell flat.

"All depends. How much you make it worth my while, how much fun you can promise me. I thought you said you were not the kind of woman who had fun."

She opened her mouth, felt the twitch of her hand wanting to slap him, the tart taste on her tongue as she wanted to light into him.

But she was stuck at the front of a parade with a hero, two scout troops, a football team, a marching band, the mayor and all Winnetka.

"I'll make it fun," she promised, but the light flirtatious tone dissolved into pleading. "I'll make it worth your while."

"Oh, Kate, you try so hard," he said, laughing. "You try too hard sometimes. You've got to lighten up. I'm not some wolf who's going to devour you."

He accepted a bouquet of flowers from a giggling matron who had run in from the curb. As the matron ran back to her family, he handed Kate the flowers, careful to lean close enough so that the mayor wouldn't overhear.

"Besides, you're making sex sound like as much fun as washing the car. That's no way to talk to a man."

Chapter Seven

This is exactly what he hated about coming stateside, Kyle thought.

A speech. Kyle didn't like giving speeches.

He looked out onto the Winnetka village green. And Winnetka looked at him.

The Boy Scouts holding the color guard of flags. The nursery school children standing in brave, solemn rows. The football team squirming restlessly. The marching band, its members dripping sweat from beneath their white-and-purple-plumed hats.

And over a ribbon-and-stake fence that snaked through the center of the green, the civilian population. A field of floral sundresses and straw hats, plaid madras and khaki shorts. Makeshift fans of magazines and rolled-up newspapers waving back and forth, back and forth. The occasional baby squawling.

Everyone waiting for him to give his speech so they could get on with the picnic.

The disappointment was nearly but not quite covered by polite attentiveness. No doubt about it, Kyle was second best—he was not the hero, the true hero, that this town longed for. That being Lieutenant Parker Cabot IV, of course.

The judgment of his audience, made in error, was exactly what Kyle had run away from, the reason he had signed up as a young man for the most dangerous work overseas.

Although Kyle would never admit to running away, exactly, from anything. Much less the judgment of small towns—in particular the small town of Brownsville, Kentucky. He had never been any of what Parker took for granted. Never had what Parker had given up. He had played center to the quarterback, the B student to the valedictorian, the best friend of his own hometown hero. The small town he'd grown up in didn't have room for a boy from the other side of the tracks. It wouldn't have "looked right" for him to take all the honors reserved for boys from "good families."

It had only been by leaving, striking out on his own, going halfway around the globe that he had found himself as a man. A man judged on his work and his merits, his courage and his strength—not on the merit of family connections that crisscrossed in a small town like an intricate spiders' web.

The judgment of these people of Winnetka didn't sting quite so much as he would have expected. He was confident of his power, proud of his accomplishments.

After all he had done, the fires he had walked through, the battles he had fought, the impossibles that he had overcome—what others thought of him no longer had the power to wound. Even a comparison to a happy-go-lucky bartender who had stolen his hero status.

Just two more hours and Kyle would be safely on a commercial jet that would hopscotch across the islands and the oceans to Sri Lanka. Within twenty-four hours, he would be popping open a beer at the Two for the Road and explaining to Parker what the word *jerk* really meant and how it applied to Parker himself.

He wondered for the hundredth time why he was doing this and he knew it was for her. For Kate. What had once been spite and pity was now admiration and tenderness; what had been irritation was now full-blown attraction.

Kyle pulled the index cards from his pocket.

He glanced back at the dignitaries seated on folding chairs. Mayor Cruikshank, the fire marshal, the police chief, the superintendent of schools, Father Ferrigan from Sacred Heart, Reverend Patton from the Winnetka Bible Church and Rabbi Nitzberg from Am Shalom.

And Kate. Nervously twisting the hem of her linen skirt and squirming from side to side in her folding chair.

Their eyes met, hers pleading.

The speech—how well he knew her thoughts— *read the speech. All right*—please *read the speech.*

She was his age. Thirty. She was a serious, good woman. She wasn't his type. He wasn't hers. But he had challenged her, flirted with her, made her think they had a deal. If he read the speech, she'd give him...everything. She had no way of knowing that he was too much of a gentleman to collect.

And then he noticed the oddly brilliant twinkle in her blue-green eyes, the flush of her cheeks that wasn't just July heat—no, she wanted him to read her speech and then she wanted to give herself to him. To think that she had been cornered into sex, coerced by duty into taking him into her bed, something she'd never in her right mind consider, but which now appealed.

She wanted him.

And she wanted him to want her enough to break down her thirty years of training in being a small-town lady. Wanted him to take the responsibility for doing something she was unsure she had the courage to do.

She was a proudly unselfish woman and didn't want her world turned upside down. And Winnetka surely depended on having its hero.

By his next words, Parker could be destroyed or he could be left alone. But, whatever happened, it would be Kate picking up the pieces.

He looked deep into her eyes. Looked at the conflicting desires. And then he looked out onto the green.

Sighing, he knew he was just like her.

At the core, some part of them both flinched at hurting others even with the truth, recoiled from taking what was theirs when it would leave others hungry.

And this crowd was hungry. And a little restless, wondering if this substitute player would run with the ball.

But he didn't care about their judgment. It was Kate he did this for. A lazy smile played across his face.

Funny how a woman who had been for so long just a photograph in a bar halfway around the world was now the center of his thoughts.

He studied his index cards.

He had to do what was best for her.

With a forceful rip, he threw away Kate's carefully constructed speech. Index card confetti fluttered to his feet.

He heard her gasp.

"I want to talk to you about bravery," he said into the microphone.

The feedback whined high-pitched and he adjusted the mike's height.

The audience snapped to attention. He was ready for them, staring into their eyes, taking the measure of each member of his audience in turn, demanding their complete attention—even if he wasn't Parker.

"I want to talk to you about bravery in the jungles of Southeast Asia. I want to tell you a real story of courage. And courage is what the Fourth of July is all about."

DAMN. DOUBLE DAMN.

Kate wasn't given to swearing but at this moment

she wished her vocabulary included stronger words. Really stronger words.

She stared dismally at the snippets of index cards that formed a paper snowdrift at Kyle's feet.

She stared at the crowd, her town's residents, their rapt expectation—little did they know their most prized ideal was soon to be destroyed.

Their hero was about to be brought down.

As she thought of the consequences, she also felt an ache in her heart. It was silly, really, but she had promised to give herself to Kyle if he would read the speech she had prepared for him.

They were both joking—a little. Both serious—a little. Obviously she was more serious than he had been. It meant nothing to him. And it meant everything to her.

Admit it. She had half hoped he'd live up to his end of the bargain. And demand that she live up to hers.

Instead, he was going to tell the truth about what happened in the jungles halfway around the world, several years ago. She knew he had a right to have the truth be known. But did he understand?

The truth would have consequences.

She looked out at her neighbors, her fellow Winnetkans, their hand-held fans momentarily stilled, their mouths agape, their children quiet. She waited for the shrieks of disbelief—no, no, Parker couldn't be such a coward! She waited for the moans of despair—this couldn't be true!

None came.

Rapt silence. Mouths open. Necks craning.

And then she started to listen, really listen.

"I was scared that night, and the other men in our squad were scared," Kyle continued. "But Parker understood what heroes have always known. A man can never stand tall again if he leaves one of his own behind. And a man who can't stand tall isn't really a man. The rest of your life means nothing if you cower in fear the one time—or the many times—fate puts another person's life in your hands."

Kate stirred in her chair and stared at Kyle's back as he went on to describe a firefight of intense ferocity. And how Parker came back, cutting through the jungle to recover his battered and bleeding comrade. And how Parker dragged Kyle back to the clearing and pulled him, hand over hand, up the rope ladder to the waiting chopper. And how, as the gunshots struck the chopper blades and the chopper spun out of control, Parker shouted these words to Kyle.

"Parker said to remember that he was only doing half the job," Kyle said. "Parker said the other half of ensuring freedom and liberty was doing the work that you of the village of Winnetka do every day. Raising the children and teaching them values. Putting food on the table. Caring for the sick and the needy. That's what he said happens in Winnetka every day. That every one of you is a hero to your hero Parker."

The crowd erupted into applause.

As she absently joined in, Kate wondered if Kyle wasn't laying it on a little thick. After all, the image of Parker hanging from a doomed chopper screaming about all-American virtues and the importance of Winnetka was outrageous and, if anyone gave it more than a moment's thought, they'd realize the absurdity of it. But the crowd was eating it up and Kyle ploughed ahead with his saga.

"And so, after the chopper went down and Parker dragged all of us to civilization—which is a long and convoluted story that would take too long to tell—I was given the privilege and honor of being Parker's friend. As his friend, I salute you. And now, I'd like to introduce the woman whom Parker himself described as the other half of heroism—Kate Lodge."

He turned, holding his hand out to her, encouraging her to the podium.

Now he really had gone too far!

She stared daggers at Kyle, who had that wicked smile on his face.

Gotcha, he communicated without saying a word.

Accepting her fate, she smiled brilliantly and stepped up to his side. She put a hand over the microphone.

"That was a whopper of a lie," she said into his ear.

"Yeah, I don't feel good about lying, but I have to admit, I did an awfully good job."

"I wanted that!" She pointed down at the discarded pieces of index card.

"No, darling, you wanted that!"

He took her hand from the microphone and pointed out at the Winnetka crowd. Clapping. Cheering. Tears streaming down the cheeks of men and women alike.

Children with their eyes wide and their thin expectations uplifted. The entire football team looking as if it were ready to enlist—if the army would take sixteen-year-olds.

And the older folks looking as pleased as punch— their own everyday heroics were being recognized and honored.

Kate knew, in her heart of hearts, this is exactly what she had wanted. She waved at her neighbors, waved at her parents and stood with Kyle, waving at her town, until the mayor stepped up to announce the picnic would be starting.

"DID PARKER GET SHOT in that jungle?" Kate asked quietly as they walked to her car, which she had parked this morning on the corner of the green so they could leave from there for the airport. No way was anything getting in the way of Kyle leaving town.

"Yeah, on the foot," Kyle said, shaking hands with Mrs. Rubin, who owned the bookstore. He added, as soon as they were out of earshot, "He shot himself in the foot with his own revolver."

"In the middle of the jungle?"

"Yeah. It was an accident. He was cleaning his gun. I had to get him out of there."

"Was there a helicopter?"

"Yes."

"Did the helicopter get shot down?"

"Yes," Kyle admitted. "But the pilot and copilot ejected safely."

"And did it take weeks to make it to safety?"

"Yes."

"And did Parker—or you—say what you said about small-town heroes?"

"Kate, you've got to be kidding me. Do I look like the kind of guy who's going to waste time with a speech like that?"

Kyle shook his head, guiding her through a crowd of well-wishers as they reached her car.

"Nobody said anything about small towns. Parker whimpered and cried for most of the time. Said he wanted his mom. And I never said anything about small towns because I don't like them. I made that part up."

Kate felt inexplicably hurt. She got into the car and switched on the ignition. "How can you not like a small town?" she asked as Kyle slipped into the passenger seat.

"Maybe saying I don't like them is too strong. I actually don't think about small towns one way or another."

"Never?"

"No. I don't think about America or what I've left behind. I don't think about the little town in

Kentucky I grew up in or the principles of freedom, liberty, democracy or apple pie. I just do my job.''

"That sounds awfully grim."

"That's a warning, Kate."

"What do I need a warning for?"

"Don't make me out to be a hero. I hate it when people do that."

"But you are. You saved Parker's life."

"And look what kind of trouble that's gotten me into," he said ruefully.

"Well, I'm about to take you to the airport and that'll be the end of all your troubles. We'll say goodbye and you can take your warnings with you."

"I don't think so," Kyle said.

He pointed out the driver's side window at the approaching policeman. Kate rolled down her window.

"What's the matter?"

"I'm sorry, Miss Lodge," Officer Kerner said, bobbing his cap at Kate and then at Kyle. "We've blocked off Elm Street, so you can't go through here."

"What about Maple?" she asked, pointing to the corner.

"That's closed, as well. You know, the picnic and all."

Kate felt her heartbeat begin to gallop. "I have to get this man to the airport," she said. "He's got a plane to catch. Can't you clear the streets?"

"I'm sorry, Kate, but the picnickers have even

started setting up on the street because the green is so crowded.''

"Okay, okay, we'll call Paul Nilson," Kate said, her thoughts racing ahead. "He's got to have a cab running. We'll walk to his garage."

"I don't think so. I saw Paul Nilson out on the grounds," Officer Kerner said. "He's out there somewhere."

All three looked out onto the green.

There was no way they would find anyone in the tangled mass of picnickers.

"How am I going to get Lieutenant Reeves to the airport?" she wailed, feeling a stabbing pain in her chest.

"Pardon me for intruding," Officer Kerner said. "But the mayor said Lieutenant Reeves was staying through the fireworks. He'll be setting off the first torch. By the way, that was an awe-inspiring speech, Lieutenant."

"Thanks, Officer."

"Did he really pull you up to the chopper like you said?"

"Yeah, he did," Kyle said darkly.

Kate closed her eyes and dropped her head back onto the headrest. Being with this man and not doing something foolish for two more hours was barely tolerable, but the whole day…?

It was a conspiracy of the Fates.

She opened her eyes to mumble a good day to the officer, who trotted off to break up a water-balloon fight between three skateboarders.

"Sorry, Kate, I didn't know anything about the first torch business," Kyle said. "But I assure you that if I haven't blown Parker's cover by now, it's not going to happen. Look what I did for the guy just now. I told nearly a thousand people he was a hero."

"Get on tomorrow's plane, Kyle."

"Don't worry, I'll leave on the first flight tomorrow, and until then, not a word about how Parker is a fraud and a coward and a sweet-talking charmer."

"Promise?"

She just didn't want to do something foolish. Something she'd regret that would make it impossible for her to be Kate Lodge. Dependable, organized, sensible, trustworthy, responsible Kate.

"If you're really worried, I can even promise I won't collect on our little deal," Kyle added, roguishly tilting his chin.

"You didn't do your part!"

"Did, too."

"Did not."

"Did, too. The deal was that I not tell the truth about Parker."

"The deal was that you were supposed to read the speech I gave you."

"The speech you gave me was a snoozer."

"All right, it might have been. But the point is that you aren't entitled to anything from me."

"Not even a thank-you?"

Kate pursed her lips tightly. And then she thought about what he had done, how he had never once said a disparaging word about Parker and made him out to be the greatest hero Winnetka had ever known.

"Thank you," she said softly.

"Thank you's are what us friends-of-heroes live for," he said genially. "Now let's go eat and torch some fireworks. I'll get a flight tomorrow."

"First thing," Kate warned.

"Don't worry, first flight out of here," he conceded. "Kate, darling, you sure do have a way of making a man feel welcome."

Chapter Eight

Kate led him back to the green on a shortcut through the Greenough family's sweeping formal garden. Standing on bleachers set up at the north end of the green, the band began to play.

"Ah, 'America the Beautiful,'" Kyle said. "My favorite."

"Don't be sarcastic," Kate warned. "They're doing the best they can."

"Did I say anything sarcastic?"

"No, it was the tone of your voice," she called over her shoulder.

"Kate, you don't know me well enough to guess when I'm being sarcastic."

"Are you really a patriot who loves his country's anthems?" she asked, stopping abruptly on the brick courtyard.

"Yeah, and I don't hear them all that often overseas."

Maybe he wasn't as much of a cynic as he seemed to be, Kate thought.

"You don't come home very much, do you?"

"I don't call America home anymore. But, no, I don't come back much. Just when they want to trot me around to see the desks in Washington."

"Desks?"

"Guys who direct things from the comfort of an office."

"Not like you."

"No, not like me."

"And where is home?"

"Anyplace the desks send me."

"Including Sri Lanka?"

"Sri Lanka, Columbia, Nicaragua, the Middle East. I've been a lot of places."

"And you saved Parker's life."

He looked away. "Yeah, I did. Although, if I'd known how he was going to tangle me up here, I might have let him rot in that jungle."

"No, you wouldn't have done that," she said, brushing aside his harsh self-judgment.

She was on to him, knew that he covered his feelings under the foolish bravery of a toughened soldier. He was a gentle and honorable man, though he seemed to want others to only think of him as a rogue.

"You're right. I wouldn't have left him," Kyle agreed. "But I wouldn't have done what he's done to you. It was a coward's way."

"How would you have done it?"

He reached out and touched her cheek. She shivered.

"I wouldn't have made any promises I couldn't

keep. And I'd keep any promises I made. You know, Kate, you're going to find a man. Another man. Much better than Parker. And you're going to have lots of children and a nice house and you'll forget all about this episode."

Kate didn't believe him—not about the kids or the house or the husband or even some distant age of forgetfulness. He couldn't fully understand how small towns operated on women her age. But she nodded her agreement because there was no reason to admit that she was, more than likely, going to be Winnetka's premier spinster.

"You have a lot of people depending on you, don't you?" Kyle asked.

"Yeah, I do."

"Sometimes you have to live for yourself."

"Is that what you do?"

He shrugged. "When I'm not on a mission, sure. On the downtime, I live for myself."

"I can just imagine the hobbies and interests that fill your days," she said, staring up at the sky. "But living in a small town like Winnetka, there's no downtime."

The band squealed through a particularly high-pitched and off-key finale. Immediately followed by a melody that had a hard time coming up to speed because the flutists had mistakenly started the national anthem. But when the flutists stopped and skipped through the first several bars at lightning speed, a fairly passable version of "You Light Up My Life" drifted through the trees.

"That was Parker's favorite song," Kate said ruefully, pausing to smell the lilacs that bordered the brick path. "They must have played it a dozen times at our prom. Just this way, too. With the bassoon just a few bars behind the rest of the band and the flutists out to lunch. We danced until midnight."

"If Parker were here, would he dance with you?" Kyle asked at her ear. He plucked a fragrant lilac bloom from a nearby tree and tucked it behind her ear. Her severe hairstyle had pulled away from its pins, and her curls tumbled across her shoulders. He liked it like that. And then he was surprised that he even had an opinion.

Kate nodded, disarmed by the intimacy of his touch.

"He was a talented dancer."

"I'm sure he was," Kyle conceded. "And I'm a terrible dancer. But just this once, Kate, just this once, dance with me."

He took her hand and threw away the long stalk of wheat grass she had been absently twisting. He drew her into his arms and she reflexively started to slip out of her espadrilles then stopped. Parker had been her height so she had never danced with her shoes on, but Kyle was just right for the too-tall Winnetka girl.

One sure, broad hand slipped to rest on the small of her back and the other welcomed her lithe fingers in his. Her breasts squeezed against his chest, but she jerked back and gave him a prim warning look and he loosened his grip. She wished he weren't so much of a gentleman as to obey and then grumbled at her wanton thoughts.

They came together on the brick-and-grass courtyard under the shade of the Greenoughs' apple trees.

Sure, he wasn't Parker. Parker had been complex steps and flashy hand-offs, Parker used to clear the dance floor so people could watch his skill. Parker had been style and twirls and snapping fingers.

Kyle wasn't going to win any awards from Winnetka's ballroom dance committee. He swayed back and forth in the most elementary two-step. But he had a natural sense of rhythm, bringing them together as one.

She gave herself to dancing, to the moment, knowing its bittersweet taste. It wouldn't last. It couldn't last.

Was he doing this just to be nice?

It didn't matter what his motivations were, she told herself. It could be beautiful just the way it was.

She wanted to remember everything, everything for the forever to follow. The music was...well, the band was trying its best. The dance was slow and aching. Its scent was green, the green of the trees overhanging the bower. Its color was sunlight, cleansing and bright. And its taste was...

"If you're thinking about Parker, that's all right," he said. "No need to feel guilty about that."

He couldn't know that Parker had drifted from her mind as a pleasant but distant memory. If anything, the smidgen of guilt she felt was that she wasn't more mournful of her fiancé.

On the other hand, Parker had broken up with her in a particularly cowardly way. She didn't owe him any romantic allegiance at all.

But she did owe a lot of people her aid. She owed them her strong sense of doing what was right over doing what was pleasurable. Those people couldn't see her in the shade of the overhanging trees, at the back of the Greenoughs' house. They couldn't know of her embrace with a stranger.

"If Parker were here, would he kiss you now?"

She caught her breath, and blinked up at him. "Yes…yes, he would."

She gulped, catching her breath as he caught her lips with his. She was surprised by the intensity of his touch, but not completely unprepared. She wanted him, wanted the taste and feel of him just one more time. The soft power of his lips.

And now she was a graduate of lesson one in how to kiss him. None of that breezy, friendly peck on the lips that she remembered from her dates with Parker. No, this was being with a man. Giving and receiving pleasure, coming to know the sensuality that masculine brought to her feminine self.

Kate could hardly believe that she was almost thirty and might as well be a virgin for all her experience. But she could make up for lost time, here in the seclusion and safety of the Greenoughs' yard because surely he wouldn't take advantage of her here.… So she could grab every bit of pleasure without paying a price she wasn't sure she could afford.

"Whoa, there!" he said, pulling away. "Not so fast."

She flushed and looked down, embarrassed. "Kate, we can take it as slow or as fast as you want," he said, lifting her chin and forcing her to look at him. "Or we don't have to do anything at all."

"But I want to kiss you. Just kiss you."

He touched her lip with his finger.

"If you're going to kiss, you have to kiss like you want it. Not like you have to, not like you're doing it on a dare, not like you're racing through, or like you're trying to get it over with so you can remember you did it."

"Then show me how."

He had never had a woman be so honest with him, place all her trust in him. It would have scared him, would have made him recoil, made him shake his head and send her chastely on her way. It would have done all those things.

The day before yesterday.

This trusting woman was beautiful to him in a way that had nothing to do with looks. He wanted her, but couldn't say why. She wasn't his type, and yet... He wanted to give her this taste of pleasure, though he knew it would be another man—someday—who would take her for his own. Kyle wouldn't interfere with that. Before Kate, he had never thought of a kiss on its own, not as a matter of foreplay, to be pleasurable.

And the kiss he had shared with her yesterday had

affected him as no wild, uninhibited night shared with a knowing and willing woman.

He had thought he had long since unlocked every sensual mystery, had figured out every sexual secret. But maybe he was going to learn something from Kate. Still...

"I've never been one for taking on virgins."

"I'm not a virgin," she snapped.

"All right, not technically a virgin. But you might as well be. I'm just saying I'm not the kind of man who's ever taught a woman anything."

"Try," she said, her opalescent eyes narrowing as she threw down the glove of challenge. "Because my only other alternative is Mr. Frumble," she said, and suddenly her voice took on a sly drawl worthy of the most delicate Southern belle. "I will have to turn to Mr. Frumble in this hour of need and ask him to instruct me on the sensual art of kissing."

Kyle felt the blood rushing to his head. He recognized that tone of voice. He felt like a fool.

"Kate, you tricked me on the porch into telling you about Parker!"

"I sure did," she said proudly. "I had to know. And you weren't going to tell me any other way because you have your own code of honor about ratting on a friend."

"So you didn't mean any of that about not giving yourself to another man. You're going to be dating before I even get back to Sri Lanka." The thought was oddly unnerving to him.

"It's none of your business whether I do or not,"

Kate said. "But the fact is no, I won't be dating. There isn't anybody here for me. Small towns don't work the way big cities do."

"Oh. I see," he said, and he did see—the unbroken vista of virtuous loneliness that would be Kate's fate. "Well, this is what we're going to do, Kate. Close your eyes and give up seeing and analyzing and rationalizing. You're good at all those things, but you don't need them now."

"All right."

She took a breath, as if she were about to dive into the deepest part of the pool. She closed her eyes, and he resisted the urge to kiss the pale eyelids.

"Stop clenching your teeth, Kate."

"Sorry."

He brushed his lips against hers, back and forth until he heard her moan, deep and inviting. They came together, and the last conscious thought he had before he lost himself in her, was that she was a very fast learner.

They stopped in a daze, in the split second before Kyle knew he wouldn't be able to control himself—or her.

She stared at him with widened blue-green eyes. "Why'd you stop?" she asked breathlessly. "Was it something I...?"

"No, Kate, it's just that I can't guarantee I'd be a gentleman if we were to do this any longer."

He meant it as a warning and yet, he could see by the way her hand fluttered to still the pulse at the pale base of her neck, that she was flattered. Intrigued. Mystified. Curious.

Funny how she was strong and confident in so many ways, and then a vulnerable innocent in others.

He felt a sudden stabbing feeling—an inexplicable anger at any man who might take advantage of that vulnerability. She didn't deserve to be treated again the way Parker had treated her. He wished he could protect her, could ensure that the man who one day claimed her as his wife and the mother of his children would be a good man. But there was no way he could do that from halfway across the globe.

As if sensing his protectiveness, she drew closer, pulling at the shoulder of his jacket, offering him her lips. Her linen skirt brushing tantalizingly close against his straining groin.

And then just as suddenly, she jerked away.

He saw out of the corner of his eye a flash of color. A boy in a bright red T-shirt, who couldn't be more than nine years old, ran out from behind a peony bush. Giggling, he skipped out of the yard.

Kate smacked her forehead with the palm of her hand.

"Oh, dear. Now I'm really in trouble."

"Who was that?"

"Alex. Little Alex Greenough. He's going to tell his mom that he saw me kissing you. Then his mom's going to tell everyone she knows on the landmark preservation committee and there's ten members on that committee. His father's going to tell everyone he works with at the bank. Then those people are going to tell—''

"I got the idea," Kyle interrupted. "How long will it take before everyone knows?"

They looked beyond the trees, beyond the Greenough house, to the green crowded with picnic blankets and folding chairs and minigrills and children dashing this way and that.

"About ten minutes," Kate guessed.

She sat down on a tiny decorative wrought-iron chair.

He didn't even try the one placed next to her, it was so small.

Instead, he crouched down and pulled the flower out of her hair. She took it and slipped it into her skirt's pocket.

She was shook up. Trembling and flushed. Her shoulders hunched and her mouth set tight. He wondered how much of it was his kiss and how much of it was the prospect of exponentially increasing gossip.

"I'm in so much trouble now," she said, shaking her head. "I've never been the kind of woman to get into any kind of trouble."

"It's just one kiss. You're a single woman. You're nearly thirty. You can do what you want."

"I'm engaged to the town hero," she corrected.

"Not anymore," he countered bluntly.

"Then I'll have to tell them that. I've dreaded it so much. I'm the kind of woman who wants to make everything just right for everyone. And now I have to go tell them that the wedding they've looked forward to isn't going to happen."

"Now?"

"Now. Before that village green erupts with gossip. We should go," she said, taking the lead on the path through the Greenoughs' patio to the front lawn that overlooked the green.

He jerked to his feet and followed, scrambling to catch up with her quick, long strides.

"What exactly are you going to tell them?"

"Sort of the truth."

"Sort of the truth?"

"Sure. I'm going to tell them everything that Parker wrote me."

He grabbed her arm and yanked her to him. "Whoa, there, Kate, that's not the truth. That's not even sort of. The truth is that Parker—"

"The truth is that Parker is a very brave and honorable man who is devoting his life to being a hero for his country. And you only kissed me in that arbor because I was so overwrought."

"I kissed you because I wanted to."

"Is that the absolute truth?"

"Yes. The absolute honest-to-God truth. No 'sort of' truth about it."

"Oh, really? I didn't think I was your type."

"Kate…"

She shook her head at his protest. "You're too much of a gentleman," she said. "Too much of a gentleman to tell a town its hero isn't worth having and too much of a gentleman to admit to a lady that kissing her was an act of charity.''

"I'm not a gentleman,'' he sputtered, but she was already halfway across the street.

"You are, Kyle Reeves," she said, shaking her finger at him. "You are a gentleman and a hero and a dangerous man.''

He shook his head and Kate nearly laughed aloud, despite the pain in her heart. She was sure that her own words had been uttered by many women before her. Along with a special, intimate invitation.

Well, she had an invitation of her own. An invitation to the door.

"I want you out of here on that next flight," she warned with her best schoolmarm voice. "And don't contradict anything I have to say about Parker.''

She left him standing on the curb, confident he would follow. And even more confident he would back up everything she had to say.

Now all she had to do was figure out how to say it best.

Chapter Nine

"...And so I must confess to you, my sweet Kate, that I could not love you more were I to love my country and my honor less."

Kate folded the letter and slipped it into her pocket, making sure not to disturb the lilac bloom that Kyle had plucked for her. She would save that—but the letter she would probably burn.

"The rest of what he writes is purely personal," she explained. "But you get the idea."

"Wow," said the fire chief.

"We feel for you, Kate," said the mayor, nodding his head sagely.

"Oh, dear," said Mr. Lodge.

Mr. Cabot opened his mouth to speak, but fell silent.

Kate's mother and Mrs. Cabot reached to clasp hands.

A crowd, drawn by her dramatic reading of the letter from their hero, surrounded the Cabot and Lodge picnic table. The young ones elbowed each other for a better look at the brave and bereaved exbride-to-be. The older ones wiped away a sentimental tear.

One teenaged girl made a swooning noise, but her mother told her to get a grip on herself. The children stared solemnly, openmouthed, uncertain what was going on but curious enough to stop playing freeze tag for a moment.

Kate figured a quarter of Winnetka's population was in the circle around her, and while her knees knocked together and her hands trembled, she took comfort in the fact that her linen skirt was long and her pockets roomy.

No one could tell just how much she was shaking with fear—somebody was sure to shout "fraud" or "liar" and then she'd really have some explaining to do.

On the other hand, she was getting it over with, and in ten minutes or less the remaining three quarters of Winnetka would know her wedding was off and that Parker wasn't coming home.

Then she would pick up the pieces.

"But can't you have one of them newfangled 'commuter marriages'?" Mrs. Maguire inquired loudly. "Surely the United States Army would let him come back on occasion. You know, he could be shrouded in secrecy and all. We'd all keep quiet when he came back."

A murmur of agreement swept through the crowd.

"This doesn't sound fair," someone said. "He's already given up so much for his country."

"Doesn't sound right," another said. "My first

cousin worked for the FBI, or at least that's what he said, and he was away a lot but always got home for holidays. Can't be much worse than marrying a truck driver. Being away for long periods and all that.''

Kate looked at her father, pleading silently with him to say something. But he simply took off his glasses and started to rub them with his sleeve.

The mood of the crowd had shifted subtly. Kate knew that soon the questions would come, harder and even more troubling.

This is what lying about Parker had gotten her.

Commuter marriage?

Coming home for holidays?

Truck drivers?

She ground her teeth.

If Parker were here she'd give him a piece of her mind for leaving her with this to deal with.

''We should simply accept Parker's decision,'' Mr. Lodge said quietly.

''Yes,'' agreed Mr. Cabot, coming to stand next to his best friend. The two older men looked decisive and in no mood for questions. ''I agree. Parker knows best. He saw the road ahead, knew how unfair it was to Kate to tie her down to a life where his devotion as a husband would always compete with his devotion to his country. I think he made the best decision releasing Kate from their engagement. And I think we need to respect Kate and Parker and stop meddling into their private affairs.''

Kate stared. It was the longest coherent string of

sentences the shy and wistful retired botanist had ever put together.

"But what about the team?" asked Joe Miller, the practical-minded quarterback.

"We'll have practice tomorrow just like every Monday," Kate said.

"But come the first exhibition game against Wilmette, we're going to lose," he pointed out, with the bluntness of a teenager who thinks his concerns are what keep other people up at night.

"Maybe this season we'll get better."

"Yeah, right. Um, I mean, sorry, Miss Lodge. This must be hard for you, too."

"What about the blood drive next Saturday?" called out an anxious voice. "We've always counted on Parker to bring people in."

"We'll still do it. In fact, this year, we need to do an even better job than last," Kate pointed out, warming to the topic. "We need to show our devotion to our neighbors, our country, our soldiers overseas. Every pint we give means life for..."

As she started the well-worn speech that she gave every year at the local churches, at the woman's club and at the Village Hall Citizen's Day celebration, the crowd began to thin.

Then, through the sea of floral print dresses and plaid shorts, she saw Kyle talking with Caroline Fleischman, his head leaning close to Caroline's ice blonde head. Caroline's eyes fluttered dramatically and she said something at his ear. Something so funny and witty that Kyle threw back his head, his white teeth gleaming, his strong jaw pulsing.

"Uh, the resources of the Red Cross..." Kate continued absently. "The resources of the Red Cross are used to help literally millions of people for whom there is no other hope...."

It was when Caroline put her magenta polished fingertip on Kyle's row of medals that Kate waded through the crowd across the village green.

She told herself it was because Caroline, as clueless as she was, might get Kyle to unwittingly blow Parker's cover. She told herself it was because she was trying to keep a town together, acting unselfishly, in the interests of her family and her community.

It never once flickered across her brain that she was acting out of an emotion so base as jealousy.

With a perfectly correct but somewhat chilly greeting to Caroline, she slipped her arm in Kyle's and half led, half dragged him into the clearing by the statue of Winnetka's founder.

"Stay away from the natives," Kate warned. "I don't want you discussing Parker with anybody. The less said the better until you get on that plane tomorrow morning."

"She didn't want to talk about Parker," Kyle said innocently. "She just wanted to see my medals. The few I didn't give to Parker."

"I'm sure she wanted to see a whole lot more."

"Jealous, Kate?"

She reared her shoulders back proudly. "Jealousy

has nothing to do with this. I'm protecting Parker. I'm protecting his family. I'm protecting this town."

Kyle lifted an eyebrow. "Selfless to the end, that's our Kate."

She colored. She had never heard the word *selfless* sound so priggish, so prim, so sour.

"I'm not selfless," she said. "I can be very selfish."

"Try me. Tell me the last time you acted purely in your own self-interest."

She racked her brain.

"I sometimes buy a paperback and go to the beach and read a book in the afternoon. All afternoon."

He shook his head and gave her the once-over with his dark blue eyes.

"That sounds positively indecent."

"It is pretty darned selfish because I should really help my father out at the hardware store he owns. And I do, most afternoons right after I finish teaching. But if it's a slow day, sometimes I'll slip out and..."

"Shameful," Kyle said with a lazy, mocking tone. "Tsk, tsk, tsk."

Kate narrowed her eyes. "You make being selfless sound like a vice."

"I'm only suggesting that you could try being selfish just once. And leave other people alone to do their own selfish things—like that Caroline woman. She just wanted to flirt," he regarded her carefully. "Kate, being selfish once in a while wouldn't mean the end of the world. So whatever it is you're thinking of, do it.''

She crimsoned.

He knew what she was thinking of.

She knew exactly what he was thinking of.

And she wanted to, really wanted to.

She felt her desire like a fire spreading from the lowest part of her belly. He would kiss her and she would be like a flame.

Even if he was leaving tomorrow—maybe especially because he was leaving tomorrow—making love to him would be the ultimate in selfishness.

But she had been raised Kate Lodge.

She eyed him coolly. ''And when would I fit in this sudden impulse for selfishness?''

''If we slip out right now, we could finish what we started up there.'' He pointed to the Greenough house. ''I could still make my plane tomorrow morning.''

''You're talking about a one-night stand.''

''I guess that's what you'd call it if you were being crude.'' He moved in closer—so close she could smell his heady scent of citrus and musk. ''I'm talking about doing…something nice. Something selfish for both of us. Something wonderful.''

''But people would talk.''

''People won't notice you leaving.''

He gestured to the crowd, the tumult of children playing tag, friends sharing laughter, seniors fanning themselves until their eyelids drooped and they napped contentedly. A pick-up game of basketball was being organized. Dads were firing up the grills. Moms were picking plastic ware out of their picnic baskets.

Maybe he was right. Nobody would notice them leaving.

Oh, how could she be thinking this way?

And then her eyes caught those of Margie Paris, staring wistfully at Kyle. Nearby were the Joyce twins, barely eighteen, giggling as they batted their dark lashes. A knot of school officials glanced repeatedly at Kate—they were clearly trying to figure out what impact Parker's absence would have. Beyond them, several other groups of people were sorting out what it all meant. April Morgan, tugging at the waistband of her too-tight jeans, boldly marched towards them.

"Oh, Lieutenant Reeves, I just wanted to tell you how moved I was by your speech."

"Thank you, ma'am. I appreciate—"

Kate hooked her arm through his and yanked him away with a firm, but cheery hello to April.

"People might not notice me leaving," she said from between clenched teeth. "But the female population would miss you dearly."

"Is that the only reason you're saying no?"

She shook her head. "No, thirty years of common sense are telling me you're trouble."

Kyle gave a courtly bow. "Why, Kate, that's the nicest compliment you've given me since we met."

"Don't get too excited. You're leaving soon. Tomorrow to be exact." She wagged a finger in his face. "And I think it's a good idea if we stick together—I don't want anybody asking you questions and I particularly don't want you giving anybody any answers."

HE FOLLOWED HER through the buffet table that had been set up by the extended Cabot and Lodge families, setting his plate high with fried chicken, watermelon, potato salad and biscuits. He sat next to her and listened with half an ear while she and a cousin whose name he couldn't remember talked about the chances for the Cubs to win the pennant. He got her a soda from the cooler under the table and made sure to come right back before she got too nervous.

Through it all he felt like a fool.

A blasted fool.

How had he ever lost control of himself like that?

If she hadn't used her very best schoolmarm voice to refuse him, he would have pressed. And he could have had her. She didn't even know how much she wanted to be made love to by him. And he hadn't realized how much he wanted her. He had come very close to breaking every personal rule he lived by.

One: Never seduce a woman who's going through a personal crisis—although she seemed to be taking Parker's betrayal a lot more coolly than he would have ever predicted.

Two: Never seduce a virgin—although he kmew that she wasn't technically a virgin, he could tell from the feel of her lips and the way her body trembled as he touched her that she was as innocent as if she had never been touched before.

And Three: Never make promises he couldn't keep.

He stared at Kate who was doing a pretty good job of explaining why the new infield lineup would make the Cubbies invincible.

He thought, *I haven't made her any promises at all.*

But she wasn't the kind of woman a man could make love to and leave. His physical needs would be sated and his emotions would roar into high gear.

He had seen it happen to so many of his buddies—a woman changed everything.

Why, just the week before he had gone to a going-away party for a Special Forces officer who was leaving the army because his new bride didn't like him putting himself into danger. The army had lost a good man. And the good man hadn't looked too cut-up about it.

Kyle shook his head. That would never happen to him. He couldn't imagine what had made him so desperate to want to bed a too-tall, too-skinny, smart-mouthed redhead. It would never happen again.

'Til the fireworks began, he made small talk with the picnickers who brought their plates to the table. He felt Kate's watchful eye, and he was careful to keep his conversation light.

After following the mayor up to the hill to light

the first box of fireworks, he made sure to come right back to Kate before she started to wonder.

He lay back in the grass at her side and stared up at the night sky. The fireworks cast an eerie light on the green, familiar as that cast by firefight. Every explosion bringing his memories of battle into focus.

They weren't all happy memories. Some were quite terrible. He would change the way he had done some things, and he was troubled by regrets, missions that hadn't gone smoothly. But in the heat of battle a man makes his choices and lives with them. He was proud of himself—he had never left a buddy behind, and that, he supposed, was all that mattered.

Trying to keep cool, he didn't notice the trembling of his hands until Kate placed her fingers on top of his. He was a proud man, he was a hard man, he was a man who had faced danger without flinching.

He didn't need a woman's touch.

But her touch felt good. It felt right. She calmed him.

He didn't move. Just let the anxiety and the barely recalled fears subside.

And then her hand moved away and he had to be satisfied with just looking at her profile in the light of cascading stars.

The fireworks concluded with a special shower of red, white and blue sparkles. Having gotten past the tension, he was able to enjoy its beauty—he clapped and hooted at the end as easily as the next man. When it was over, the Winnetkans rose from their seats, wiped the grass from their pants and skirts, folded their chairs and called for their children.

"I'd suspect you need some sleep," Mr. Cabot said to Kyle. "How 'bout if I drive you to the airport tomorrow morning?"

"Yes, sir, that'd be nice."

"We'll miss you, son."

"Yes, sir, I'll never forget my time here."

As Mr. Cabot leaned upon his arm for the walk home, Kyle knew he wouldn't forget.

LATER, KYLE SAT ALONE in Parker's room, where the Cabots had put him up. The bed had a brass headboard and an antique quilt. The desk displayed an assortment of pictures of Parker in various moments of triumph.

Parker certainly had been the golden boy of Winnetka.

Parker in his football uniform being carried on the shoulders of his classmates. Parker arched skyward as he threw a javelin. Parker scoring a goal in soccer, the ball appearing to fly even in the still picture.

And there were pictures of Kate—mostly yearbook shots—with carefully styled hair and a fixed, somewhat dazed, smile. A few pictures showed the couple together, dressed in high style for a yearly prom or mugging for the camera in jeans and T-shirts.

He looked out the window, tree branches pressed against the panes like a child's face at a toy store's window.

He was wistfully glad she hadn't said yes. It wouldn't be Kate, the Kate he was beginning to think he knew, to do something so impetuous, so base and so raunchy as a one-night stand with a man she'd never see again.

Somehow it made him proud of her that she'd refused him.

And then he heard the gentle tapping sound at the window. He opened the window.

Kate, wearing shorts and a T-shirt, had climbed across the arbor separating the Lodge and Cabot house.

"I just came here to talk," she said, as he helped her into the room. Her stern gaze challenged him to disagree.

He didn't. He'd heard that line before, he thought as he closed the window behind her.

And he knew that when he had been rationalizing why it was a good thing that he and Kate hadn't made love, it had been just that—rationalizing.

Chapter Ten

"I came here to thank you," she said.

He leaned against the windowsill and watched her pace around the room, rearranging the things on the desk, wiping some dust from a picture of her and Parker as children.

Her opal eyes skittered about, as if she anticipated being ambushed by paparazzi whose photos of her indiscretion would splash across on the pages of next week's *Winnetka Talk.*

He should make it easier for her, take her into his arms, make it seem like seduction was his idea.

His and his alone.

But he liked watching her, slowly dancing back and forth, though she could scarcely know the alluring, erotic effect she had on him.

Her hair, all the sexy miles and miles of it, spread across her back like a field of red. Her mouth, too big and pouty for someone so prim and proper, had been touched with the lightest, most ladylike pink lipstick. She wore a tiny dust blue T-shirt that showed off her high, tiny breasts and her hips were hugged by a pair of faded denim cutoffs. Cut a little too high for anyone but a woman with a great pair of legs, which she had.

"Thank me for what?" he asked, enjoying himself.

He was a man who got what he wanted so easily. Having to pace himself to Kate's rhythm was a new, exotic pleasure.

"Thank you for preserving Parker's reputation," she clarified.

"You're welcome." He nodded. "And I'll make sure he thanks me personally as well when I get back to Sri Lanka. Right after I explain to him what a jerk he's been. To all of us."

She stared up at him, her green eyes darkening to blue. "You won't hurt him, will you?"

The words were said without any irony or blood lust. He marveled at her loyalty. If he were her, he'd want to land the first punch himself. But then, everything he knew about her suggested that loyalty was her greatest virtue.

"No, I won't hurt him," Kyle assured her reluctantly. "But he'll understand I'm not happy. Same effect. Less bloodshed."

She smiled, her full, sensuous mouth trembling. "Poor Parker doesn't like to disappoint people."

"I suppose that's why we're here now," Kyle agreed. He stepped away from the window. He watched her eyes scan the room like a trapped animal looking for an escape route. Or a woman who couldn't decide between following the dictates of her heart or her head.

She wanted him, she couldn't want him, she wouldn't let herself want him. He could see every emotional twist and turn course through her body.

"Is thanking me all you came for?" he asked lazily, touring the room, tightening a circle around her.

"Oh, no. I, um, wanted to warn you to not let Mr. Cabot drive you to the airport. He'll get lost— he always does. He doesn't have any sense of direction. Let my dad do it."

She stepped two steps away. He walked forward two steps. She backed into the bookshelf and quickly reached to right a toppling soccer trophy.

"I'll keep that in mind," Kyle said smoothly. "Don't drive with the Cabots. Got it. Is that all?"

"Yes," she said, sliding out from between him and the bookshelf. "Yes, that's all I wanted to tell you."

Kyle put his hands on his hips. "Why didn't you just phone me?"

"Because I didn't want Mrs. Cabot listening in. She always does. It would embarrass her to be reminded that Mr. Cabot can't follow directions and that she can't do it because she lost her license after the surgery on her corneas last year."

He jerked his head toward the window. "So, instead of calling, you climbed out of your window and through the branches of a tree into my bedroom," he queried. "Won't Mrs. Cabot hear us now?"

"She takes out her hearing aid at night. Parker and I went back and forth across the arbor all the time when we were kids."

"Why?"

"I guess we thought it was cool doing something our parents didn't know about. We read together late at night, I did his math homework a lot, he typed my papers all through high school. We never…"

"Never what?" he asked, moving closer to her, close enough to smell her scent scrubbed fresh with just a hint of flowers and talc.

Her eyes widened as she sputtered a denial. "Never…never made love here. Well, actually, we did make love. But not here. In this way. Oh, why am I telling you all of this?"

She twirled around and found herself locked in his embrace.

"You're telling me these things because you have something on your mind," Kyle said hypnotically, leaning forward to brush his lips against the frothy copper curls at her forehead. "Something you don't want to talk about. Something you think you can't say. So I'll say it for you. You want to make love to me and you want me to know that you haven't got a lot of experience at it and you're a little afraid."

She reared back her shoulders and gave him her most withering glare. "That's not it," she lied. "I don't want to make love to you."

"Then why'd you put perfume on before you came?" he demanded, brushing his face against her cool, wet, fragrant hair. "Lily of the Valley. Nice. Fresh. Summery."

"Huh?"

"Lily of the Valley perfume."

"How'd you know?" she demanded, wiggling out from between him and the bookshelf.

"Just because I live in a jungle, doesn't mean I'm an animal."

"Oh, I get it," Kate said imperiously, clearly trying to recover from the embarrassment of having been found out. "You've had so many women, you can identify perfumes by name!" she exclaimed. "If there were a word for men who sleep around, you'd probably think it was a compliment."

"I'm experienced," he admitted, though he knew that his actions of the past few years had put him a little out of practice. "But, face it, Kate, would you climb over here if I weren't so experienced?"

He put his hands around her waist. Such a tiny waist, he marveled. He had to hold himself back from taking her right now. But she needed to be coaxed, to be persuaded to listen to the part of her that knew how much she wanted him.

"You want this, Kate, and you're asking me. You want to be somebody else for a few hours. You want to put aside being everybody's big sister, everybody's baby-sitter, everybody's teacher. You take care of a whole damned town, and for one night, you'd like to let them take care of themselves. You want to be somebody else—you want to be yourself."

"Oh, really?" She tried for sarcasm. Instead, she choked on her own righteousness and her words came out as breathless and seductive as a Las Vegas showgirl.

"Kate, let's be who we really are for just a few hours," he said, running his hands underneath her shirt to her taut belly. He loved the feel of her silky, sun-kissed skin. He wondered if he could ever get enough.

"No heroes, fake or real, no good little girls. Just one man, one woman," he whispered. "Kate, that's all we need tonight."

SHE SHOULD PROTEST, push him away, she should fling up the window and get out now. Instead, she leaned her head forward onto his bare chest and moaned softly—expressing a pent-up need she had never known was there.

As his fingers slid under the hem of her T-shirt, her nipples stood erect against his callused hands. A fire storm of heat spread throughout her belly.

"Oh, Kate, feel what you do to me," he groaned.

With a hand on her buttock, he pressed her to the bulge straining his button-fly jeans.

His raw urgency frightened her. There were no tentative kisses backed up with promises of lifelong devotion. No Mother-may-I? touches and please-oh-please! declarations of respect to come the morning after.

This was a man whose hardness was a measure of his wanting.

He knew what he wanted. He knew, as no man had ever, exactly what she wanted. And knew how to give them both so much pleasure that she would be shamed, wanton and dependent on him. He might be promising only a few hours, but those hours were sure to transform her, to change her tastes from the innocent to the sensual.

From dependable Kate to some kind of...

She jerked away from him, nearly knocking over the moth-ridden giant panda that Parker had won at the state fair years before. She charged for the window.

"I hardly know what you're talking about," she said primly. Too primly. Nope, she couldn't be prim enough, Kate decided as she escaped, slipping from limb to limb over the arbor and sliding into the safety of her bedroom. She shoved the window shut behind her and breathed a sigh of relief.

And regret.

He hadn't tried to stop her. Hadn't even said a word. Had just smiled that devilish smile that was going to haunt her for the rest of the night. For the rest of her life.

She looked around her spare, feminine bedroom.

Her sanctuary.

Her prison.

Life sentence.

And no time off for good behavior, she told herself as she looked back through the leaves to Parker's window. She couldn't see anything. He wasn't pining for her. A man like that didn't need to. She yanked the curtains into place.

Thank God tomorrow he'd be gone. Back to Sri Lanka, halfway around the world. Surely far enough away to stop being a temptation. She touched the lilac bloom that wilted on her dresser. The memory of this night would fade as surely as the flower.

She found a book on her nightstand, and settled in. She had a feeling she wasn't going to get a decent night's sleep.

THE NEXT MORNING, Kate awoke late. Ten o'clock. She hadn't slept that late in years. But she hadn't gone to bed until dawn, which wasn't the sort of thing she did, either.

Running a quick mental check through her morning routine, she put on her jeans and oxford shirt, picked up her whistle and clipboard from the dresser.

Although tired, she was pleased with herself. Disaster had been averted. Tragedy brought to a close. Peace and order restored. Kyle Reeves was gone. Life would return to normal. Hopefully she could put this episode behind her.

She glanced at her watch. The plane had probably already left.

Her eyes were shadowed from sleeplessness, but otherwise she was the same Kate as she had been the day before. Or, at least, almost the same Kate.

She had a two-hour practice scheduled for the

football team and then the monthly meeting of the Winnetka library board, of which she was chairman. Later, she would stop by her father's hardware store to help with inventory.

Oh, and she reminded herself that she'd better start making phone calls to get volunteers to man the remaining open shifts of the blood drive in addition to her list of phone calls to cancel the wedding. She hoped that with grace and poise she would be able to deflect intrusive questions everyone would have.

"You look perky this morning," her father commented from over his newspaper as she made herself a cup of coffee. "Considering all the trauma of the past few days."

"I'm...better," she said.

Her mother and father exchanged a worried look. Kate knew they were thinking she would have a tough time recovering from the blow of having her engagement to Parker broken. As far as they knew, the love of her life had just put the brakes on their future and Kate should be devastated.

She couldn't confide in them, although she'd truly like to, about her real feelings—

She wanted Kyle. Badly.

She would have a tough time recovering from Kyle. Even though Kyle had done nothing more than kiss her and touch her....

Better not think about it, she commanded herself, reaching for the front section of the newspaper.

She was a strong woman with a clear sense of

right and wrong. And though she was flexible enough to know that the right thing in one situation often was the wrong thing in another, she trusted her moral compass to tell her the difference.

And the compass needle had pointed in one direction—get out of his arms!

It had taken hours to calm herself, to flip sightlessly through her book, to restlessly toss and turn until nearly first light, to reassure herself that she wasn't throwing away her only chance at happiness.

There were other men in the world, and other men in Winnetka—Mr. Frumble couldn't possibly be the only single male over twenty-five. After all, she had been an engaged woman before, off-limits, but now she was free.

Free to date, although dating sounded pretty grim, from the descriptions given by her girlfriends.

Still, it was the only way to find a man.

And she needn't limit herself to loving a man from her hometown. There were men in the surrounding small towns of Northern Illinois. Safer men. Men of responsibility and upright moral character. Gentlemen.

And even if there weren't, she could live without a man in her life. She had her family, her friends, her work—it was so much more than most women got out of life, how could she complain?

She sat at the table and took a blueberry Danish from the serving plate. It tasted like cardboard but her mother stared at her so intently that she took another big bite as if she relished the taste of it.

"So, how was it getting Lieutenant Reeves to the airport?" she asked with forced nonchalance.

"I don't know," her father replied.

Kate felt a sudden choking sensation. She gulped her coffee. It was too hot, but she barely noticed the burning liquid firing her throat.

"You mean, you didn't take him?"

"No, the Cabots thought they'd drive him out," Mr. Lodge said. He stared at his daughter over his spectacles. "Is something wrong?"

"I WANTED TO GET out of Winnetka as much as you wanted me to get out of Winnetka," Kyle reassured her. "Maybe even more."

They sat together on the wicker swing on the Lodges' porch. A dismal pair. Kate was ten minutes late to practice—she was never, ever late—and still she couldn't manage the energy to get up.

Kyle tugged at the constricting tie of his dress uniform. He had driven with the Cabots for nearly an hour and had done nothing more than gone in a wide, convoluted circle around the town's borders.

Kate and Kyle shook their heads in unison, both regarding themselves as the only injured and aggrieved party.

"Why did you go with the Cabots? I told you they'd get lost."

"Your father went over the directions to the airport with them. He said it was all right. He couldn't find his glasses so he couldn't take me."

"He puts them in the silverware drawer of the

dining room armoire every night. He should have known better than to send you with the Cabots.'' Kate shook her head again. Suddenly she panicked. ''They didn't…ask you anything, did they?''

''Mr. Cabot asked me if Parker was happy. I said yes. They didn't ask me for details. The rest of the time we talked about the chances of the Cubs winning the pennant. Don't people in Illinois have anything better to talk about?''

''They weren't more curious about Parker? I mean, if my son's best friend came home from a far-off land, I'd want to know everything.''

''They weren't curious about him at all,'' Kyle snapped. ''Look, Kate, there's not another plane until tomorrow morning. If you just get me to the airport, I'll wait for the plane there. I can't get a room at the hotel—there's some convention of meat packers—but I can find a comfortable chair.''

''Overnight?'' Kate asked, horrified. Her natural instincts about how to treat a guest made her recoil from the suggestion.

''I've slept in foxholes. I've slept in jungle rot. I've slept in the middle of a desert sandstorm. Airports can't be much worse. Besides, it seems to be the only way to ensure that I get there on time tomorrow.''

''I have one other suggestion,'' Kate said uncertainly.

''What is it?''

''Why don't you stay here one more night?''

''Here in Winnetka? Aren't you afraid that I'll

suddenly forget myself and blow Parker's reputation? Aren't you afraid some seductive female is going to use her wiles to get Parker's secret out of me?''

"No, I'm not afraid of any of that," Kate said decisively. "Because you're going to stay with me. I'll make sure you don't say a word."

Kyle's eyes narrowed. "I'm going to stay with you the whole time?"

"Yes," she said, relieved as she sensed his assent to her plan and unexpectedly thrilled about the prospect of another day with him. "Now, come along. We've got a football practice and then a meeting at the library, and I'm supposed to line up volunteers for the—"

He grabbed her arm and she was instantly brought to her senses. He gave her the once-over, paying particular attention to the way her blouse fell at the neckline. How the delicate bra beneath hugged her diminutive curves! How her nipples stood erect, her breasts full and aching for his touch!

She wondered if it would be a better idea to give him a pillow, a blanket, and drive him out to the airport right now.

"The whole time with you?" he asked, his lazy appraisal making it quite clear what he would like to do with some of that time. And it didn't involve good deeds, hard work or community relations.

"Almost the whole time," she corrected, rapping his fingers as if he were a disobedient schoolboy. "You have to sleep."

"You haven't forgotten last night, have you?"

Abruptly standing, she collected her clipboard, backpack and whistle. "I haven't forgotten last night. As I recall, you made me an offer and I declined."

As she hustled him off the porch and into her car, she wondered how long she could hold out against her own desires.

And if he would even ask her again.

Chapter Eleven

"We're never going to win, so what's the use of playing?" Joe whined.

A quick check of his teammates' grim nods made it clear that he was speaking for all of them. Even with pads and jerseys, they looked smaller and more vulnerable than ever. Friday's preseason exhibition game against the Wilmette Huskies looked like just another setup for humiliation.

Kate's heart ached for her young players, but somehow she had to persuade them they were not quitters.

"Why don't we forfeit?" Linebacker Tommy Flickinger suggested, his grin showing off a tooth knocked out in one of last season's games. "Then we wouldn't even have to show up. We could have a party instead. You know, have an *un*victory party."

Several of his teammates grunted their approval. Tommy Flickinger always had good ideas for a party.

"Guys, guys, this isn't the right attitude," Kate pleaded, glancing at Kyle.

Perhaps he had a football speech tucked away in his brain that was just as inspiring as the one he had given on the village green. But he merely stared at her laconically, his jaw clamped shut, his jacket slung over the back of his shoulder. His black aviator glasses gave him a remote, unapproachable look.

Then she remembered she had told him not to say a word, had repeated that instruction half a dozen times in the car on the drive over to Winnetka Central High School's campus.

He was taking her commands seriously. Or maybe he was punishing her with his complete obedience to her express wishes. She was beginning to see that he wasn't the kind of man a woman should order around.

He took off his shades. The morning sun shot through his blue eyes, and he had a steely gaze that Kate hadn't seen before. She felt disconcerted and covered her feelings by loudly taking attendance. She already knew every player was here. Every time she glanced at Kyle, she noted he was studying each of her players in turn—his cool, hard gaze evaluating them.

When his gaze settled at last on Kate, her pulse quickened and her thoughts were drawn to the moment that he touched her....

Bad idea, thinking of last night, she chastised herself.

Praying that no one else could tell the effect he had on her, she wiped some sweat off her forehead with the back of her hand and tried again.

"Boys, we need an attitude readjustment before Friday," she said.

"And just what is the right attitude?" Joe challenged. "Parker Cabot is never coming back to coach this team and we're never going to win. So what's the attitude we're supposed to have? No disrespect to you, ma'am, of course."

She ground her teeth. "We're supposed to get up off the grass, wipe off our negative feelings and try our hardest at the next game."

"We did that every game last year and we lost again and again and again," Joe said, defeated. "Every year we lose. I don't think I want to do it again this season."

"Just because Parker's not here to coach, you guys think you're automatic losers?"

Nods all around.

Kate bit her lip—the question had been rhetorical.

"I'm not saying you're a terrible coach," Joe said, although it was sounding to Kate exactly as if he were, which was too bad, because there wasn't a man, woman, child or dog in Winnetka who would take her place.

"You're great at the encouragement part," Joe said.

"And you set Jimmy's arm right on the field when he broke it at the Downers Grove East game," Billy Sholten said.

"You threw a great end-of-season party," Tommy offered. "And you helped me with my math homework so I wouldn't get thrown from the team 'count of grades."

"And you understand the rules of the game, which is better than the last guy they had coaching us."

"Then what's your problem, guys?" Kyle asked mildly.

Kate looked back at him. That mildness was deceptive, and she nearly warned the boys.

"We lose. We're losers. That's our problem," Joe said sullenly, standing up to Kyle.

Joe was the tallest, broadest, most muscular boy in Winnetka—and he was only sixteen. He was used to being intimidating when he wanted to be, which wasn't often since he was quite sweet by nature. As sweet as a sixteen-year-old boy can be.

But Joe had met his match.

Kyle stepped over to Kate's side, chin raised so that he reached his full height—towering a good half foot over Joe.

Joe stepped back.

"Why don't I watch you play?" Kyle said, more a challenge than a suggestion.

"Why don't you just do that?" Joe replied, hanging on to his pride with a shrug.

Kate shook her head at this display of testosterone.

She blew her whistle and the rest of the team picked up their helmets and got ready for the lineup.

Joe joined his teammates at the scrimmage line. Offense wore blue jerseys, the defensive players of the team were wearing red.

"All right, guys, let's show Lieutenant Reeves our best!" Kate encouraged. She glanced upfield. "Jack, you're not feeling sick again, are you?"

"He's just adjusting his uniform," Kyle said. "Do you do that at games?"

"Do what?"

"Ask these guys whether they're all right."

"As a matter of fact, I do," Kate replied indignantly. "I care deeply about my players."

"Well, stop asking them. Nothing makes a guy feel worse than a woman asking him—in a loud enough voice that others can hear—if he's all right. Makes him feel like a baby."

"So what am I supposed to do? Jack's mother called me this morning and told me he had a stomachache, and I promised to pay special attention to him."

"Here's how you do it," Kyle said, cupping his hands on his mouth. "Hey, Jack, when you heave, make sure you do it on Joe! Okay?"

Jack gave him a thumbs-up signal.

Joe reached out to Jack and cuffed him playfully on his helmet.

Kate's mouth dropped open. "That's disgusting what you just said."

"That's how you deal with teenage boys," Kyle said. "They're almost men, you know. And men are even more disgusting."

Biting back a retort, Kate blew the whistle and play began. She felt funny with Kyle near, felt defensive about her coaching. She had done her best, though she was an English teacher by training.

She explained that Tommy couldn't run very fast because he had twisted his ankle five weeks before.

Kyle didn't say anything.

She said that Bob sometimes held back from the scrimmage because he was a timid boy by nature.

Kyle shook his head, didn't want to hear it.

She explained it was only Rory's first year playing and that Michael was actually trained as a figure skater.

Kyle remained silent.

She watched her boys grunt, groan, shove and run. They went through several plays before Kyle roused himself to speak.

"How come Joe takes all the runs?"

"Because he's the quarterback and he's good at it."

"But you don't make touchdowns."

"That's because he's not good at avoiding the players from the other teams. He runs straight very well. He can't make sudden stops and direction changes."

"And his teammates aren't used to playing," Kyle added. "They're used to holding back and waiting for Joe to do all the work."

"Maybe," Kate conceded.

She wasn't about to tell him that everything she knew about coaching football had come from the textbooks that the previous coach had left in the equipment room when he resigned.

With nonchalance that belied his decisiveness, Kyle looked across the track to the school's lawn. The maintenance man drove the tractor-mower back and forth in perfect, straight lines. As she followed his gaze, Kate had a funny feeling that Kyle was about to destroy all the fine straight lines of the lawn.

And their game.

"Get on out here, Joe!" he yelled.

Joe got out from under a tackle and looked at Kyle doubtfully.

"Where're we going?" he grunted.

"Go with him," Kate encouraged, having no idea what Kyle had planned but curious to see what Kyle had in mind. And certain that her team couldn't do much worse than to follow Kyle's instructions for a practice.

She and the team watched as Joe, helmet still strapped in place, followed Kyle to the manicured front lawn of the school. As the two approached, the tractor-mower came to a halt. After a quick, but animated conversation with the maintenance man, Kyle turned and walked back to the field, leaving Joe behind. And seemingly unaware of the flurry of activity behind him.

The maintenance man fired up the engine. With a roar and a cough of thick black exhaust, the mower chased Joe across the lawn, around the science lab and through the Future Farmers' garden plot before disappearing behind the building. Leaving a dazzling wake of shorn grass in a crazy-quilt pattern.

Kate stared. She felt her boys standing behind her.

"Ohmygosh," Tommy said.

"Wow, look at Joe," Jack said. "He can really run."

"He'll get a workout," Kyle assured her. He walked past her to the team, which stood open-mouthed in awe. "Now, boys, we'll play some football. Stop staring at Joe. He's doing his warm-up and you're going to do yours. You've got a game to win on Friday."

"SORRY I TOOK OVER," Kyle apologized as Kate drove them to the library. "I have a habit of doing that."

"It's all right. At least, it was once I got over being defensive."

"You've done a good job."

"You're just saying that. I'm actually not a very good coach. But I'm the only person they've got," Kate said. "You make me think we have a chance at winning. Some of those plays you taught the boys were pretty sophisticated. Using Michael as fullback was inspired."

"All that training as a figure skater's made him pretty quick on his feet," Kyle mused.

"He actually did a triple souchow jump over Jack to get that last touchdown."

"Is that what that was? I thought he was just showing off."

After a half hour of being chased by the mower, a humbled and exhausted Joe returned to the scrimmage. The team had never played better.

"Don't get cocky," Kate warned. "You're only their coach for today."

"You'll have to write me about the game," he said, and then suddenly his expression darkened. He had never, ever asked a woman to keep in touch. When he left a place, he left it for good. Never kept a woman waiting for him. Never missed anyone. And never looked back. He wasn't sure how he felt about looking back for Kate.

"We've never won a game so don't hold your breath," Kate advised, unaware of his distress. "And without Parker coming back, I don't know how long the school board will pay for team equipment and league fees if we don't do better."

"Then you'll have to win. At least once," Kyle said absently.

"Easier said than done."

"You've got the raw material. You can make them into a winning team."

"By myself?"

"Why, Kate, are you asking me to stay?"

Kate looked at him. Their eyes met and Kyle was the first to blink. He pointed out a parking spot in front of the library. Kate pulled in.

"No, not at all," she said. Just in case he was still thinking about his question. "No, I'm not asking you to stay. But I'll send you a postcard. Promise."

He grimaced, hating the part of himself that looked forward to that postcard, that wondered if her script would be loopy or scrawly or tightly drawn. Would she include anything personal, or would she be as snippy in her letters as she was in person? Would he be able to catch her scent on the paper?

Hell, he hadn't gotten any exciting mail from stateside in years, except for the Victoria's Secret catalogs that every man looked forward to getting.

Bad habit to start now—waiting for that mailbag.

He followed her into the library.

"Now don't say a word," she said. "This isn't like football. I know what I'm doing in a library."

"Hey, I read books. Newspapers and magazines, too."

"Name the last one you read where the woman didn't have staples across her stomach."

LIKE ALMOST EVERY other day in her week, Kate ended the day with more things on her to-do list than she had started with. Even though she'd been running nonstop from morning.

"Are we finally done?" Kyle asked, lying down on the couch after reassuring himself that no one else was at the Lodge house. He could let go, be himself—not just a friend of the local hero. He slipped off his shoes and crossed his hands behind his head. "This being Kate Lodge is pretty exhausting."

"You're done for the day," Kate said. She sat down on the velvet-covered chaise and pulled out her date book to write herself notes on things she must do tomorrow. "You came up with enough ideas at the library meeting to keep me busy for weeks, and the blood drive is never going to be the same. I thought I told you to keep quiet."

"I don't take orders very well," he said, closing his eyes.

"How'd you survive the army?"

"By being the best at what I do," he said, without a smidgen of boastfulness. "I get my assignment, I pick the men I want and I get the job done. I do it well enough that the army leaves me alone otherwise."

"How'd you ever end up with Parker?"

He opened one eye and then shut it. "Only once, and it was a mistake. He charmed me into letting him hop along for the ride—and I ended up...well, you know the story. Just remember my speech on the green. Just reverse the roles."

The grandfather clock in the hallway counted out four chimes. Kate smacked her hand on her forehead. "I forgot!"

Kyle startled, his reflexes as finely honed as a predator. "What's wrong?"

"It's already four o'clock. I forgot I was going to help my dad with inventory at the store. The meeting went so long that it must have slipped my mind."

"I'll do it tomorrow," Kyle said shaking his head and lying back down.

"You won't be here tomorrow, remember?"

She had grabbed her purse, shoved her feet into her shoes and was halfway to the door when he quietly dropped a bombshell.

"What if I stayed?"

"You wouldn't," she said, feeling a sudden sickening in her stomach. A flipflopping of joy and horror. Joy to be with him, horror that he would still be here. "Not another day, Kyle. You have to go."

"Why? I haven't got anything waiting for me. Except Parker, who'd probably be just as happy to wait another day for his punch in the jaw."

But it wasn't Parker's jaw that was worrying her. "Look, Kyle, we've been very lucky that nobody's been more curious about Parker than they have been. Nobody's asked you any questions you can't dodge and you haven't taken it into your head to blow Parker's cover story. We've just been lucky. Why don't we just let me do the inventory and you get on that plane?"

He opened his eyes and gave her a wicked grin. "You sound pretty anxious to get me out of here."

"I'll do anything to get you to go."

"Anything?"

She gulped. Did that arched eyebrow mean what she thought it meant? Funny, the idea of "anything" didn't seem so unappealing. In fact, it sounded pretty good—and she felt her conscience rev up its engine.

It was wrong to make love to a man you didn't have a committed relationship with. Or to have a brief, quick affair—oh, admit it, sex just for fun. But she'd be doing it for a good reason. A very good reason.

She swallowed at the dryness of her mouth and bit her trembling lip. The day had been building to this. All the sidelong glances and the shared smiles. She knew that now.

"Anything," she confirmed.

He got up in one swift motion and she thought surely this was it.

He'd sweep her off her feet, carry her upstairs and...

Her heart pounded wildly.

He walked past her to the front door.

"You know, Kate, you're the kind of woman who would probably lie back, grit her teeth and think of England," he said, referring now to the age-old advice given to reluctant brides. He tugged at the doorknob. "And you don't live in England!"

He slammed the door behind him and left Kate standing on the hallway runner.

Damn that man! she thought, staring at the front door. *If he walks back in here, I'm going to tell him no dice. I've come to my senses. I've gotten a grip on myself. I'm not lowering my standards for some mercenary with great biceps and a charming smile.*

She stood there a long time waiting, but he didn't come back.

Chapter Twelve

"Six thousand four hundred and twelve, six thousand four hundred and thirteen, six thousand four..." Kyle paused. He stared up Kate's long, long legs to the ripped denim shorts. He gulped. And then, with a defeated sigh, dumped a handful of one-inch bolts on the floor.

"Aw, Kate, now you've made me lose my place. I'll have to start all over again."

"Sorry."

Kate crouched down to help him pick up the bolts he had lost. Her hair cascaded like a coppery, curly waterfall onto his face. Suddenly, he wanted so much to smother himself with her scented hair and pull her to him—but he had learned his lesson with Kate.

She talked like a woman with a halo attached to her head, thought like a woman with a halo attached to her head, walked like a woman with a halo attached to her head. And should be treated like a woman with a halo attached to her head.

He grabbed a handful of bolts and shot her an unforgiving look.

"Sorry," she repeated, glancing back at her father, who was laboriously counting and recounting paint liters in aisle one. "It's nearly seven o'clock. I've been looking for you for three hours."

"Scared I was telling everyone that Parker is a no-account gin-joint owner?"

"No, I was actually scared I'd hurt your feelings."

Kyle took the rest of the bolts from her slim, warm fingers. He regarded her thoughtfully.

"Why, Kate, if I didn't know any better, I'd think you had feelings for me," he said. Then adding slyly, "But I think it's a better guess that you're worried I won't leave tomorrow morning if you don't keep an eye on me."

"Will you?" she pleaded. "Will you leave tomorrow morning?"

"Don't worry, I will." He leaned forward, so close that he could kiss the freckles on her nose. He knew he was ruined forever for sophisticated women with made-up faces. Soft, innocent freckles would turn him, although perhaps not with the power that Kate did. Prissy attitude and all. "Kate, don't worry, I'll leave," he repeated, surprised at how the words made him ache. He looked down at the bolts scattered on the floor. "But I want to help your father finish up before I go. It's what Parker would do."

"Parker never helped at this," Kate said with

barely there bitterness. "He was always too busy with football and being class president and all."

"Well, it's what Parker would do if Parker were the hero we want him to be."

Kate pulled out the bin next to the one Kyle had been counting from. Kyle sorted the contents of his bolt bin on the floor, starting over at the laborious count that made the hardware store's accountants so happy. *Maybe the accountants should be forced to do this,* he thought.

"Kyle," Kate said quietly.

He ground his teeth. He had recounted—what?—two hundred of these bolts, and now he'd have to start over. Again.

"Yes?"

"Did you mean what you said about England?"

He racked his brain. "Ah, yes, England," he said, remembering the barb he had thrown at her when his frustration level had reached its dangerous peak. "Well, do you?"

"Do I what?"

"Do you think about England when you make love?"

She crinkled her nose. "Not England, particularly."

"Maybe I should put the question another way," he said. "When you make love, do you give yourself completely to making love, or do you grit your teeth and do it because you think you're supposed to do it?"

"I...I better not answer that."

The hot blush on her face was graphic answer enough. He knew he should stop this conversation, go back to counting things, make a few jokes to get her mind off the topic. Hell, to get his mind off the topic.

Still, he felt for this woman more than he could express to anyone, including himself. He wanted her to be happy, to not doubt herself the way she did. Not doubt that she was a beautiful, passionate woman who could make a man happy for the rest of his days. Not doubt that she would have the love she deserved and needed so much.

Someday.

But not from him.

Couldn't be from him.

Because he wasn't the kind of man who stuck around, made lifelong promises, or even wanted a house, wife, children and picket fences.

And she was wife material—no doubt about it.

"Kate, there'll be a man who will make love to you, and you'll feel it," he said, with unexpected tenderness choking him. "Stars will explode and firecrackers will pop off in your ears, and you'll let go of yourself. I don't know, Kate, you're so strait-laced ordinarily, I bet you'll turn out to be the kind of woman who hollers loud enough to wake the neighbors."

"Really?" she asked, a playful smile turning her somber face to bright.

He would remember that brightness to the end of his days. It ached to know that brightness would belong to another man. A man he had to sell Kate on, so she didn't get confused and give her heart to Kyle.

She was the kind of woman who gave her heart to only one man—and the only reason why she could let go of Parker with such grace and poise was because, whether she knew it or not, she had never given him all of her love. Parker had fooled all of Winnetka, but never Kate. She had always known the truth, even if she wouldn't admit it. Kyle admired her for that, for having kept her vision clear.

And yet, she would do anything to help others keep their innocent regard for their hero. She knew that civilians needed their heroes and their innocence. And so he respected her for her misguided attempt to preserve Parker's reputation, even when he personally thought Parker deserved nothing but scorn.

"Really, Kate, you'll find that happiness. And the man who does that with you is going to love you the next morning. And the next morning after that. And all the mornings of your life stretched out before you. You deserve that and it will come."

"Honest?"

Her lip trembled just a bit, and he had to stop himself from reaching to still it and to cover it with his own.

Watch it, Kyle, he told himself.

"Honest." He nodded, though he was too jaded

a soldier to believe in justice for the innocents. She could just as easily have no other man.

"Honest." She repeated the word softly, caressing it like a lucky charm that she could hold in her hand to remind herself that the best days of her life were still ahead.

"Kate, we both know that man isn't me. I'm just not a forever kind of guy. I never have been. I never will be."

"I didn't say..." She looked away.

He wanted her, so deeply and sharply that it took every ounce of his strength and self-discipline to not reach for her. She deserved a bridal bed laid with linen and lace—but the dusty linoleum floor of her father's hardware store would be just fine, for Kyle.

He would soften her fears with kisses, gentle feather strokes of his lips on her face and neck— reassuring her, calming her, readying her. And then he would deepen his touch and his kisses, teasing her to want more until she became as fervent as he.

Then it would not matter where they were—the bridal bed would be no better than the floor.

Halo on her head, he reminded himself harshly.

There was a discreet cough.

Kyle jerked his head around.

"I forgot my count," Mr. Lodge said from behind the latex paint display counter. "I think I counted ten of the sea foam green semigloss but then I think I added them to the buttercup yellow semigloss. I'm all confused now."

Kate scrambled to her feet. "Dad, why don't you

sit down for a few minutes?'' she suggested, guiding her father to the stool by the cash register. ''You've been working all day. Can't you take a break? The lieutenant and I have got everything pretty much under control. Right, Lieutenant?''

Kyle looked carefully at Kate's father, wondering just how much the older man had heard. Or seen. But the poker-faced Mr. Lodge blandly stared back at him.

''Maybe I am a little tuckered out,'' Mr. Lodge said. ''Lieutenant Reeves, can I entrust my store to you and Kate?''

''Yes, sir, I think you can,'' Kyle said, coming to attention.

''Well, I think I'll go home then.'' Mr. Lodge sighed heavily. ''I'm awfully sorry I got so confused. Make sure you get every one of those inventory sheets filled out, Kate. The accountant needs them first thing tomorrow morning.''

He shuffled out of the store, leaving Kyle to wonder if he was imagining a new limp in his walk. Kate locked the door behind her father. She looked at Kyle, worry clouding her eyes.

''He's fine, Kate.''

''Do you really think so? He looks so tired. I wish I could take over the store for him.''

''You pretty much have. He's left us with a lot of work.''

They looked around the store. Every square inch of the place was crammed with tools, gardening supplies, bicycle repair kits, carpentry and electrical necessities.

"No monkey business," she warned. "We've got work to do."

"Yes, ma'am," Kyle whispered under his breath.

FIVE HUNDRED and forty eight, five hundred and forty nine, five hundred and...what is that terrible noise?

Kyle rolled over in Parker's childhood bed, reached up to the nightstand and clamped his hand down on the offending alarm.

The room quieted—except for the infernally cheerful racket the birds were making outside. He cautiously opened his eyes. He looked at the window.

Morning, and she hadn't come to him. It had all been a dream. A delicious dream.

The reality was he had waited. She hadn't come.

They had finished inventory at a quarter to three. Both had been exhausted, and although Kate had managed to reconcile the inventory sheets, Kyle felt his brain had shut down. He'd been incapable of any kind of thinking—would have clutched if someone asked him the name of the first American president, the five Great Lakes or the states with the greatest number of electoral votes.

He had felt this way occasionally at the end of grueling missions, but had always been confident that an instinctive survival sense would guide him as surely as a compass needle.

And he had always been right.

But he'd never been with Kate.

They'd walked down the empty Winnetka streets. Kate, being Kate, had made them wait for the light to turn green even though at 3:00 a.m. there hadn't been a car in sight. They had lingered at the window of the toy store because Kate was looking for a gift for her cousin's daughter.

She'd drawn closer to him as they'd passed through the woods surrounding the playground, but he hadn't taken her hand.

Kyle hadn't trusted himself to touch her, even when she'd directed him to a shortcut over a log bridge on a gurgling brook. He knew he should have held his hand out to help her across.

But the same part of his brain that had kept him alive in so many hopeless situations was also the part of his brain that didn't reflect on whether his base passions were right or wrong.

If he'd touched her, he'd have seduced her under a canopy of trees, the moon and the stars their only light.

With the remaining shred of decency he possessed, he wouldn't allow himself that one touch and he wouldn't push them both into something that would fulfill them physically but cause Kate any regrets.

She said goodbye awkwardly at the door of her house, clearly confused by the mixed signals that he had been giving.

His implacable frown. His arms crossed over his chest. And yet, his eyes hungrily raking over her body. His voice tender, but his words final. "I'll get on that plane," he said. "And rest assured, Parker will regret having gotten you into this mess."

"No," she said, touching his lip. He flinched, not trusting himself to feel her skin on his.

She drew back.

He wished he could explain. He knew he couldn't. She wouldn't understand.

"I'm glad Parker isn't coming back," she said wistfully. "If he wouldn't have been happy, it's better that he broke it off now."

"But his method—"

"Wasn't very gentlemanly," she said, finishing her sentence. "But I got to meet a real hero."

He grimaced. He realized how little he liked the term—especially as it applied to him.

"I'm not talking about heroism in battle," Kate said. "I'm talking about heroism at the hardware store."

"Huh?"

"I've never met anyone else who would finish the inventory in one night. You worked hard—and now my dad doesn't have to get up early to finish," she added. "You know, you're also a hero to the football team. We might, just might, win against Wilmette on Friday. Can you imagine how happy those boys will be? And the library board..."

"Kate, no, stop," he said, cutting her praise off more harshly than he meant. "Let's just leave it at good night."

He didn't want to know. Didn't want to hear what

he had done. Didn't like the words of admiration. She made him feel as uncomfortable as when he had to pick up the worthless medals that desks always handed out.

It was the same as having to visit people he'd rescued—they clutched his hand and called him hero and he didn't like it. Not one little bit.

He left her there on the sidewalk, opening the unlocked Cabot door and giving her only the most casual wave goodbye. He was going to be on that plane in little more than six hours.

And he'd go on with his life—the way it had been. He'd do his missions, until one of them cost him his life. He'd take a woman—only a willing, experienced one—when the need got too great. He'd work at rekindling a passion for curvy blonde party girls and ice-cold beer.

And he'd put this behind him.

Someday he'd chalk up his interest in Kate to jet lag or pity or boredom or something in the water.

He'd gone upstairs, gotten out of his clothes, set his alarm clock and tried to sleep. And every time he'd started to relinquish himself to the darkness, he'd thought he heard a noise at the window.

Kate!

He would have to refuse her, he'd thought as he'd gotten up in the darkness. Or maybe he wouldn't. Maybe he couldn't. He'd opened the window.

And every time he'd opened the window, he'd found tree branches. The wind had swiped them against the pane. He'd looked across the arbor at

Kate's dark window. She was probably already asleep. And here he was, like a Romeo—or worse! a Juliet—waiting for love to come to his window.

The last time he'd slammed down the window with more force than he intended. Getting back into bed, he'd tried to focus on sleep. And had found himself counting—the residue of hours of inventory work. Counting was terrible, but it was better than thinking of her.

Then his mind had wandered, not to numbers but to the feel of her hand in his, to the way her nose was covered with freckles or the way her too-square jaw set with determination when she knew what was right and wanted it done.

He'd slept and awoken many times to think that he had heard her scratch at the window. But morning proved that she had never come—he stared at the clock. Seven-thirty. He verified the time on his endurance watch.

Mission: get to the airport.

Odds: seemingly impossible.

He stared at the window.

Priority of Mission: highest.

Consequence of failure of mission: falling in love.

He was going to get to that airport in time for the 10:00 a.m. flight if it killed him.

Just as he was pulling on his pants, the phone rang. He stared at the nightstand phone. He let it ring once more.

Maybe she was calling him.

Ring.

He shouldn't pick it up. It would interfere with the completion of his mission if she asked him to stay.

Ring.

He gulped and cursed a blue streak, words he had erased from his vocabulary in the genteel Winnetka atmosphere.

Ring.

He gave up and answered.

"Yes?" he asked cautiously.

The line was thick with static.

"Kyle, is that you? It's Parker. What are you doing in Winnetka? I thought you were coming home."

Kyle felt the rush of blood to his temples. His right hand clenched reflexively into a tight, white-knuckled fist.

"Parker, you son of a—"

"Kyle, how is Kate taking all this? Is she going to be all right? I feel just miserable myself."

"Well, you should feel miserable," Kyle snapped.

"I've hurt the woman I love more than any other woman on earth," Parker added.

Kyle didn't have an immediate answer to that.

Chapter Thirteen

Kyle recovered sufficiently to give Parker a blistering dressing-down that he promised was only a taste of what was to come when he returned to Colombo.

But after slamming down the phone, Kyle was running late.

Have to make that plane, he repeated like a mantra.

He threw jacket and tie over his shoulder and struggled with his duffel's zipper all the way down the stairs. In front of a beveled mirror in the Cabots' front foyer, he flung down the bag and fought with the top button of his dress shirt.

Out of the corner of his eye, he saw Mrs. Cabot in the library, stacking the boxes containing Parker's—er, really, *his*—medals.

"Mrs. Cabot, what are you doing?" he asked, abandoning his efforts at making himself presentable for his travel on official army business.

Surely he had a few minutes before he really had to leave. Kate's father was driving—getting to the airport was a sure thing. He could afford a moment of compassion for Parker's mother.

Funny, he had always had a policy of butting out of other people's business. Kate had introduced him to a bad habit—caring about others.

Mrs. Cabot looked up at him with reddened eyes. "We need more space in the library so I thought I'd put these in the basement."

"Oh," Kyle said, adding tentatively, "I suppose that might be a wise thing to do."

"I thought I heard the phone ring," she said, steadily gazing at him. "I hope you don't mind that I listened in. I only heard a little bit."

Kyle swallowed. Kate had warned him that Mrs. Cabot eavesdropped on the telephone.

But even if she were on the line for less than a minute, she must have heard words that couldn't ordinarily be part of a Winnetka matron's vocabulary.

"I'm sorry, Mrs. Cabot, I didn't know."

Suddenly he wondered just how much she had heard.

"You don't have to tell me anything that Parker wouldn't want me to know," she continued, looking back down at the stack of medals. "But how is my boy? How is he really?"

"He's fine," Kyle said cautiously. "He's happy. He's doing what he's best at." Which was true.

"Is he in any trouble? Other than with you. I got the impression from the words you used that you and he aren't the best of friends anymore."

Kyle thought remorsefully of the words he'd used

on Parker. He was surprised Parker's mother wasn't more outraged at the heap of abuse he had rained upon her son.

"Uh, Mrs. Cabot..."

"Is he in trouble?"

Kyle scrambled. "Ma'am, the Special Forces unit is actually a very safe part of the army. In fact, safety is their motto, and Parker is a very careful—"

"Cut it out," she snapped. "Just tell me honestly that my boy is not in any kind of trouble. If he is, I'll personally drive a stake through the heart of anybody who's fool enough to mess with my boy. If he isn't in any trouble, I'll leave Parker be to whatever life makes him happy."

Kyle drew a sharp breath, thinking he had seriously misjudged the strength of this petite, seemingly frail, woman.

"He's running a gin joint in Colombo," he admitted, relieved to finally tell her the truth. After all, if lying to civilians is bad, lying to a buddy's mother had to be the worst sin a soldier could commit. "He's got the most popular place in town." And that, of course, was no lie.

She smiled, eyes sparkling with happiness.

Kyle had a feeling that she knew what really made Parker happy. And it wasn't being a hero.

"Has he got friends?"

Kyle relaxed. "Lots of them, Mrs. Cabot," he assured her, relieved to be telling the truth. "He's not just charming, which you know, but he also comes through for his buddies. People know they can depend on him. No matter how bad your day goes, if you stop off and have a drink at Parker's, he'll manage to find that silver lining to your own personal dark cloud."

"He was always like that."

"It's a nice trait to have. Why, just a few weeks ago, a new recruit, awfully homesick, came to Parker nearly in tears and..."

They drifted to the couch and for the next few minutes, Kyle told Parker's mother the truth about her son. About his good points, mostly.

And Parker did have his good points. Quick to loan money to a friend, just as quick to forget that money if repayment looked to be a problem. He kept a guest bedroom ready for any lonesome stranger passing through Colombo without a bunk. Honored every man's birthday with a drink on the house and an eloquent toast—for some, he was the only one who remembered. Always there with a shoulder to cry on or just an ear to listen to another man's troubles. Made living far from home nearly bearable for a lot of men simply because he brought everyone together, made them feel part of a community—just like he had done in Winnetka.

Sure, Kyle had to leave out a few parts where Parker had acted foolishly or selfishly. Explaining the medals was a little tough, but Mrs. Cabot assured him that she had suspected as much all along—although her husband was completely clueless, and she thought he should be left to his illusions regarding his only son. She hoped that the whole town would gradually come to forget Parker and then she could quietly explain the real story.

And, of course, they agreed that Parker hadn't treated Kate very well at all.

"She'll feel obligated to take care of us," Mrs. Cabot mused dejectedly. "And the horrible thing is, we'll need her. I wish we weren't such a burden to her."

"You're not," Kyle assured her. "Kate loves you. She loves everyone in this town. She'll take care of you and she'll do it happily."

"But will she have a chance to find love for herself? You know, a family to call her own? A husband, children, her own house?"

"I'm sure she will," Kyle said, and felt a sharp pang as he knew that the man who would give her those things wouldn't be him.

A glance at his watch told Kyle that he'd better say goodbye. He had just under thirty minutes before his flight. And he had kept Mr. Lodge waiting long enough.

"Mrs. Cabot, is there anything you'd like me to tell Parker when I get to Colombo?"

"Tell him to stop sending me these medals," she said. "And tell him whenever he wants to come home he can. We don't need him to be a hero. He can just be our son. We both love him very much and want him to be happy. Wherever he is. Whatever he's doing. He thought we couldn't live without a hero—but we don't need him to lie. And he could call once in a while, you know."

Kyle nodded and gave Mrs. Cabot a gentle squeeze on her shoulder. "I'll tell him that," he said. Right after he wrung Parker's neck.

Outside, Mr. Lodge was waiting, leaning against the drivers' side door of his Pontiac. He nodded at Kyle and slid behind the wheel. Kyle threw his duffel in the back seat and took one last, lingering look at the Lodge house.

Then he banged his forehead with his open palm.

"What's she doing up there?" he demanded of Mr. Lodge. The older man sighed heavily.

"We've patched this roof too many times," he explained. "Kate said she could get the whole roof done before nightfall. There's a mighty big storm coming. Didn't you hear about it?"

"And let me guess. Parker was going to reroof your house when he got home."

Mr. Lodge nodded solemnly.

Kyle looked at his watch and then at Kate, who was poised on the crown of the roof, yanking up the old shingles.

She wore a bikini top and a pair of cutoff jeans. She didn't so much as glance his way, but he could tell she was struggling.

He also knew she was a strong, determined woman, and if she wanted to reroof the Lodge house by evening, she would get it done.

Her back would ache for days. Her delicate hands would get blisters on top of blisters. Her face would get a nasty sunburn, no matter how much sunscreen she slathered on. She'd have splinters and bug bites and calluses and scrapes. And that's if everything went well.

Kyle felt a familiar tug at his heart. He had never left a buddy behind, never abandoned an injured comrade, never come back to base without everybody he left with present and accounted for.

The sight of Kate up on that roof was as wrenching as if he were watching a buddy caught in the terrible cross fire of heated battle.

He closed his eyes and tried to will himself to get in the car. *Just get in the car and go,* a sensible voice whispered in his ear. *Leave this small town and that woman behind. Do it, Kyle,* he told himself. *Get in the car and get to the airport. Gotta get to the airport!*

"Aw, hell!" Kyle shouted, defeated, grabbing his duffel from the back seat. "I'll take tomorrow morning's plane."

As he strode towards the Cabots' house to change, he barely registered Mr. Lodge's satisfied grin or the openmouthed stares of the children playing kick ball in the neighbor's yard.

DAMN HER SOARING HEART, Kate thought, watching Kyle run inside the Cabot house with his duffel. One more day? Two days? Certainly he wouldn't stay even a week, but admit it, she wanted him to stay for every minute he could spare.

Wanted him? Yes.

Loved him? She could hardly imagine that to be possible, but if it was true, then she would have to hide her love, keep tight control on her feelings, and when he finally left, she'd have only the love and the memories to last her a lifetime.

She'd have a secret, to share with no one.

In a town where no one else could keep a secret.

She swiped away the tears on her cheeks, the ones that had splashed on her face as she heard him start to leave. She had done an uncharacteristically sloppy job ripping the old shingles off the roof. But now she leaned back on her feet and regarded the roof's peak thoughtfully. What had been the start of a miserable day was now a bright, sunny vista— because he was staying.

Of course, she couldn't let Kyle know she felt this way. If he did, he would tease her without mercy.

Or worse, he would be on his guard to be a perfect gentleman. A sort of rogue with a halo on his head, ugh!

When Kyle climbed up the ladder on the side of the roof, he wore a white T-shirt, his jeans and some work boots Kate recognized as her father's. His muscles were taut and tan. His thighs strained at the soft denim. His hair glistened like gold kissed by the hot sun.

She had to turn away. Her nipples tingled and tightened against her cotton bikini top as she remembered his callused hands upon her flesh. Her breath quickened as she thought of his manhood straining against her fingertips. She was under his spell, but she had to fight it. She wouldn't let him see how he affected her.

Luckily, years of being ladylike had made her as highly disciplined in her arena as Kyle was in his.

"How could you possibly miss that flight again?" she asked, ripping out a black patch of shingle with a single, blistering tear.

If he was expecting sweetness and fawning, he gave no indication of surprise.

"If you want me on that flight so bad, get off the roof and drive me," he replied coolly.

"I have work to do."

"I'm here to help."

"I don't need your..." Their eyes met. She couldn't bear the intensity of his steel-blue gaze, but she couldn't look away.

"We both know you do," he said.

She looked down at the shingles and plywood beneath her feet.

"Fine," she said at last. She pulled an extra roofing hammer from her work apron and handed it to him. "Make yourself useful."

With as businesslike an attitude as she could muster, she showed him the spots on the roof where the underlying plywood would have to be replaced, the parts where the leaks had been so bad that tar would have to be slathered on for extra protection. Of course, every shingle on the Victorian house would have to be removed and replaced by the new ones that had been delivered to the curb by the building-supply company that morning.

"Still want to stay and work?"

He crouched on the roof. "Sure I do."

"Then let's get to it."

"Maybe you want to hear what I have to say first. I talked to Parker this morning."

Kate felt the roof begin to move from beneath her feet.

"Parker?"

The roof was definitely swaying.

She didn't even mind when Kyle took her hand and steadied her, sitting her down next to him on the roof's peak.

"He called from Colombo."

"What did he say?"

"He said he knew that you would find your happiness in the coming years and that you were a kind and beautiful and strong woman and that he admired you a lot."

Kate shrugged away his hand. "Kyle, I haven't known you for very long but I think I know you pretty well," Kate said. "You're lying. Tell me the truth."

"Okay," Kyle conceded. "He feels miserable and guilty and homesick as all get-out. He's hoping you and I will forgive him."

"He always did feel miserable when he did something wrong," she said. "He does have a conscience."

"He should try feeling bad before he does something wrong. It would be more effective that way."

"Is he coming back here?"

"I don't think so."

"Probably for the best."

"Really?"

"Really, and you can tell him I forgive him."

"You do?"

"Yeah, I'm frankly glad we're not getting married," Kate admitted. "And not just because Parker would have been unhappy."

"You would have been unhappy, too?"

"Maybe. I might not have known whether I was happy or whether I wasn't. I didn't know what love was…" Her voice trailed off and she suddenly remembered herself, remembered that her feelings weren't meant to be shared.

She stood, carefully planting her feet on the shingles. "We've got to get this roof done by tonight. It might rain hard, but if the sun is hot enough this afternoon, it'll melt down the tar and the roof'll hold."

"Kate, I have something else to tell you," Kyle said. "Mrs. Cabot knows. She listened in."

"Knows what?"

"Knows all about Parker."

Kate looked at Kyle thoughtfully. "Then you're getting on that plane tomorrow if I have to strap on your seat belt myself."

KATE'S BACK HURT. She couldn't bend down, couldn't move without searing pain coursing up to her arms. Those arms hurt, too, especially her right one. She didn't think she'd ever be able to lift a pencil again, much less a hammer.

Getting out of the shower, she regarded her hands

thoughtfully. She had always thought that her hands were her best feature. After all, her legs were too long and skinny. Her skin too freckly. Her nose too thin. Her eyes too changeable, going from blue to green and back again. Her hair too frothy with coppery curls—especially in this humid summer weather.

Unfortunately, her two best features weren't looking so good. Tar stuck up under her fingernails that just wouldn't come out. Cuticles ripped on so many fingers. A big black splinter on the left hand and a row of hammer blisters on the pads of her right hand.

She rubbed the steam off the bathroom mirror and shook her head at her sunburn. How many times had she stopped to put on that sunscreen? And still here she was, red as the stripes on the American flag. She gently touched the skin on her shoulder.

"Ouch!"

Sunburn, bug bites, scrapes, blisters, muscle pulls.

But the roof was finished.

And she had spent the day beside Kyle.

They hadn't talked much, except for the occasional grunt of effort or a comment about the heat. Hadn't touched—except the odd moment handing each other a nail or passing a plywood board.

When Mrs. Lodge had brought out a tray for lunch, Kyle had taken his plate to the shade of the apple tree in the backyard saying he didn't want to dirty the inside of their house. Kate had stood in the kitchen, eating a sandwich and finishing the phone calls that canceled her wedding.

She was pleased that the caterer would send back her deposit, disappointed that the florist had already ordered the hundreds of roses. Kate had asked her to deliver them, when they came, to the seniors home on the outskirts of town. She certainly didn't want to ever see those flowers herself.

Kyle had taken his shirt off after lunch. She had thought she would do something completely silly like faint at the sight of his taut muscles, and she had bitten back a demand that he put his shirt right back on.

But she couldn't do that to him.

It was hot. Very hot. Even she could feel it. The heat. In her stomach, through her legs, rising through her body.

Ladies didn't sweat, they glowed.

And Kate was glowing.

Maybe this was a heat, a glow, that didn't come from the sun or the burning tar of the shingles.

It came from being around Kyle. And it would never be quenched.

Around seven o'clock, they finished the last eaves of the front porch—after the sun had gone down, and Mr. Lodge had taken the dishes back into the house from a quick sandwich they had wolfed down for dinner.

She was still hot.

She was...well, hot.

The rest of the job went quickly, but not quickly

enough for Kate. Cleaning up the lawn where they had dumped the old shingles, washing the tools that were black with tar, wiping the pitch from wherever it had dripped. Kate was so aware of him, she barely knew how to do her work.

She was fooling herself if she thought she was all common sense and decency, all responsibility and dependability.

Why, she was just like any other woman.

She wanted Kyle and she was a wanton fireball.

Luckily he didn't seem to notice. Simply finished the work, looked long, hard and proudly at the Lodge roof, made a mild comment about the surprising lack of clouds in the sky and said a courteous good-night.

As he trotted up the steps to the Cabots' front door, she felt so bereft that she stood for several minutes just staring at the house.

That's when she got her brilliant idea.

SHE LOOKED AT HERSELF in the bathroom mirror but even with the steam softening her features, she wasn't sure he would want her. A lobster red freckle-faced flat-chested gawky woman of thirty.

She opened the medicine cabinet, pulled out a bottle of perfume and regarded it thoughtfully. Lily of the Valley.

No, this perfume was for summer picnics, Sunday baptismal parties and the hospital's annual fundraising dinner.

She rummaged around, found a sample vial of

Forbidden that a saleslady at Marshall Field's had foisted upon her weeks ago when she had stopped in to buy a Father's Day present.

Before she could think better of the idea, she poured the contents down her neck and rubbed it into her flesh.

Ouch! She winced. *Stuff must contain a lot of alcohol.*

She swiped her eyelashes with mascara guaranteed to lengthen and thicken. She put on her usual ladylike pink lipstick since she didn't have anything else. And then she powdered her nose. A lot. But she didn't look any better—just like a lobster with powder. So she washed it off.

He'd have to take her the way she was.

And if it were pity that moved him, so be it.

But she wanted more for her memory box than a brief kiss in the Greenough backyard or on the mud-soaked field outside the airport.

She pulled out of her chest of drawers an ivory bra-and-panty set that had seemed very risqué when she had bought it. Lace. All lace.

And then, because she didn't have anything left to lose, she put it on. Trying not to feel silly. Ivory looked awfully pale on fire engine red skin. She carefully slid a clean shirt and shorts over her tender body.

She slid her window open and, ignoring the pain shooting through her muscles, climbed over to Parker's window. Knocked twice. Waited for what seemed like forever. Kyle opened the window, held his hand out to her and closed the window behind her.

He didn't look particularly surprised to see her.

Kate stood in the middle of Parker's familiar room and looked back at Kyle. He wore nothing more than a wicked smile and a towel wrapped around his hips.

"Hello," he said.

Then silence.

So, he wasn't making this any easier for her.

She took a deep breath. Femme fatales did it. Sassy women did it. Sophisticated women did it. Sexy women did it.

But Kate had no idea how. She licked her dry lips and wrung her hands. "I, er, I came over to…"

"Thank me?" Kyle supplied.

"Yes," she said gratefully.

Now her courage left her; all thoughts of being a seductive, go-get-him kind of woman flew out the window she had just climbed in. She wanted out, back to the cloistered safety of her bedroom. Quick. Before her galloping heart exploded, before her trembling breath quickened to full-blown hyperventilation, before her shaking legs just collapsed right out from under her.

"You wanted to thank me," Kyle said, walking steadily closer to her. "And you wanted this."

She gulped. Then looked at the bottle he held up in his hand—after-sunburn lotion.

She smiled tentatively. Maybe he was going to make this easier for her. She might even get through this with some semblance of having acted pretty much like a lady.

"Oh, yes, of course," she said, reaching out to his hand. "Thank you."

And then his towel dropped to the floor.

Chapter Fourteen

He stood before her, proud and hard. At ease with his body, comfortable with his nakedness. His was a soldier's body, tough and lean, wasting not an ounce or an inch to fat.

His body told the stories of his battles and his wounds. In addition to the tiny pale scar beneath his eye was a larger jagged break in the perfect smoothness of his latticelike stomach muscles.

A lady would look away, change the subject or ignore the obvious nakedness of the gentleman in front of her. Under no circumstances would a lady stare. But Kate did anyhow.

"Wow," she said softly.

"Kate, darling," he drawled easily. "When you give it a try, you're surprisingly good for a man's ego."

Kate jutted her chin upward so there'd be no mistaking where her eyes were focused. On his face. Much safer that way.

His eyes twinkled mischievously and a wicked

grin spread across his face. If safety was what she was looking for, she wouldn't find it there.

"It's all right to keep looking," he invited.

"I've seen a man before," she said tartly.

True enough. In a way. Why, just last month a girlfriend had thrown a bachelorette party for another friend—there'd been lots of giggles when the male stripper was doing his act. Still, he had left his G-string on.

And, of course, she had seen Parker. Sort of. Parker had always assumed that she was too much of a lady to want him to stand as proudly as Kyle stood before her. And, when she was with Parker, she had thought ladies never wanted to look. Or touch. Or want.

"All right, I'll confess. I haven't done a lot of looking," she added weakly. "Actually, I've never done this kind of thing before."

He plucked the top button of her shorts and stepped back to regard her appraisingly. She felt wet with excitement though he didn't touch her, stood a full foot away from her and had his hands crossed firmly over his broad chest.

She really hadn't done this kind of thing before and she was sure that it showed.

"You might be the first woman who's ever said that to me and meant it."

"You do this kind of thing all the time?"

"Used to," he said evenly.

"Not anymore?" she asked, feeling a sudden jealousy.

"No, Kate, not anymore. And the army puts me through a physical after every mission—so you don't have anything to worry about."

"Oh."

Then she had one of those forehead-smacking insights—she hadn't even thought about the consequences of making love to him. She had just been indulging in plain, old-fashioned jealousy.

She opened her mouth, started to speak and then sharply pursed her lips.

Maybe this wasn't going to work, after all, she thought. Parker was the one who had always taken care of protection.

"If you're going to plan a seduction, you should remember the details," Kyle advised. Then he gestured to the nightstand.

She wasn't so much of an innocent that she didn't recognize the tiny square plastic package.

"It looks like you've taken care of the details just fine," she said, affecting a sophistication that they both knew she didn't possess.

She turned away from him to buy more time, but he stepped forward. Without catching her in his embrace, he kissed the exposed skin of her neck. His kisses were cool and dry and then burned more deeply than the sun.

She turned around to him, uncertain. Her yearnings and desires and love were at war with years of training as a lady. Her eyes sought out his reassurances and she found them in his velvety soft blue eyes. He would take it slow, he would be gentle, he would love her fully, deeply and completely.

Just for one night.

And since he wasn't the kind of man who could give her anything else, that would have to be enough.

He pulled out her T-shirt from the undone waistband of her shorts and stepped forward, putting his foot deliberately between hers.

She moved her legs apart to accommodate him. Heat stole into her lower half.

Now was her last chance to escape, the last chance to make a semigraceful exit.

But she didn't want to go anywhere.

"Kate, I'm not the kind of guy who makes promises I can't keep," Kyle whispered at her ear, his breath hot and sweet. "And tonight you must know that I'm not making any promises at all."

"I know," Kate answered, putting her arms around his neck. "I want you on that plane tomorrow as much as you want to be on it."

"Then why? Why this? Why me?"

"I don't know," she said, lying. She knew exactly why she wanted this, could admit it in her heart, but was too proud to say it to his face.

She loved him. Would love him tonight, and when he stepped on that plane. Would love him though she wouldn't know what dangerous mission he was on, though she would never see him again.

The sensation of love was thrilling and she longed to share it. But she knew if she confessed her feelings, he would see this as neediness. He would think she would try to trap him here in Winnetka. Or worse, his honor would not let him take advantage of her by making love to her tonight. And she would never persuade him that it wasn't taking advantage.

He peered at her from beneath heavy-lidded eyes, demanding the truth.

And so she told him an answer that was only partially a lie. "Blame it on Parker, blame it on Winnetka, blame it on thirty—but I want something for myself! I want this, Kyle, truly I do." She said it with enough conviction that he was satisfied.

Still, he gently touched her cheek, looking for one last promise that he wasn't stealing her virtue.

"Kyle, we both know why I came here."

"I suppose we do," he said with uncharacteristic tenderness. Kate guessed she was glimpsing the true heart of her hero.

He flipped the skin-care bottle up in the air and reached behind his back to catch it without looking.

"How 'bout a back rub, Kate?"

She smiled the smile of an adventuress poised on the brink of a new and thrilling experience.

Was it the right thing to do?

For the first time in her life, she didn't answer that question with her head.

Tonight it was her heart's turn to reply.

"Yeah, how 'bout that back rub?"

He helped her out of her T-shirt and shorts. She didn't wince—too much. The pain wasn't bad until he fingered the lace of her bra, and the nipples of her breasts betrayed her. Then it wasn't pain, it was heat. And it wasn't heat from the sun. It was from Kyle.

"Sorry," she said.

"Sorry for what?"

She felt a red-hot blush. As if a sunburned lobster could get any redder.

"For...well, my..."

"Breasts?"

"Yeah. For..." She stumbled over the words. "For my breasts."

"Oh, darling, you don't know the first thing about the male of the species," Kyle said, drawing a lazy pattern around her nipples. Only making the problem worse, as far as Kate could tell. "If your nipples didn't get hard, if your skin didn't tingle, if you didn't get wet, I would think I wasn't a man. But when you respond, you make me feel like this...."

He grabbed her hand and wrapped her fingers around his manhood.

She gasped and he loosened his grip, thinking that he had hurt her. He wondered about the blisters she had chalked up today, though she hadn't complained once when they were working.

"Kate, sorry, if I hurt you in any..."

She shook her head, keeping her fingers firmly around his shaft, and he felt the throbbing of desire. If he didn't watch out, he would lose control of himself.

"It doesn't hurt," she said. "It's just it's all so, so new."

"Come on, let's get your sunburn taken care of," he said, biting his lip hard to keep from exploding with the longing and tenderness that melded with his animal needs.

He pulled her fingers from him, as reluctant as she was to let go of him—and turned her around. He slipped the clasp of her bra and released her breasts. They were full and strained against his palms. She moaned softly, whispering his name.

He pulled her panties, bringing them down around her ankles, noting the sweet honey scent that rose from her core.

She kicked the skimpy lace under the bed.

"Let me look at you," he said. "It's my turn now, Kate."

She turned around, arms crossed in front of her with endearing modesty. He shook his head and pulled her hands to her sides.

"I said it's my turn."

Her body was as firm as an athlete's—he remembered she said something about running several miles a day with the football team—but her skin was smooth, really smooth.

Her breasts were high and her stomach flat, with the untried, coltish quality of a woman who hadn't yet borne her first child. Still, there was a softness that came with age. She wasn't a seventeen-year-old hard body. She wasn't like the silicone-enhanced party girls Parker hired to work in his club. She wasn't as perfect as an airbrushed Playmate—but her imperfections only made his longing more vital and urgent and real.

The dusting of freckles across her stomach seemed enchanting. The bright red tan lines at her shoulders, back and legs evoked his tenderness. The scrapes on her arms showed her strengths as well as her weaknesses, in a way he'd never seen in any other woman.

"You're beautiful," he said softly.

And he meant it.

"I'll do," she admitted.

"No, Kate, you really are beautiful."

She didn't challenge him—he hoped he had persuaded her. Because, by the end of the night, their only night for this lifetime, he hoped to show her just how beautiful she was. That knowledge would be the only thing he would leave her.

At his direction, she lay facedown on the cool, soft cotton sheets and he sat astride her buttocks. Careful not to put all his weight on her. Careful not to irritate her glowing red burn.

He squirted some lotion on his palm and rubbed his hands together to warm the lotion before putting his fingers firmly on her shoulders.

"Aaaahhh," she moaned, at first in startled chill and then relief. "That feels good."

"You've got quite a burn," he observed.

"I kept slathering on sunscreen, but obviously not often enough."

He rubbed the soothing lotion into her skin, and when his hands began to dry, he poured more onto his palms. He kneaded her shoulders, drawing the tension and strain out of her muscles. And yet, his experience taught him that she was simmering, ready to boil.

He rubbed the crisscross of muscles on her back and, shifting his weight, molded the flesh of her buttocks. She arched and her flesh rippled beneath his fingers.

He slipped his fingers to her soft, wet womanhood.

"Hey, I don't have a sunburn there," she protested lightly.

"Want me to stop?"

"No. No, don't stop."

He turned her over, and scanned the length of her body with his eyes. She was ready. Ready for him. Her nipples were hard, her stomach muscles rippling in anticipation, her thighs clenching and releasing.

And yet, her eyes darted away when he looked at her.

He used his hand to touch her, to coax the pleasure of flesh until she was ready to cry out for him.

She had to be ready in her head to give herself completely to the senses.

He squelched his own needs and gave her an encouraging and tender smile. He soothed her stomach with the lotion and caressed the smooth, silky flesh that met the triangle of fine coppery hair. She moaned and squirmed, and he knew he would bring her to the brink if he wanted.

And he wanted.

But he wouldn't do it. Not yet.

He splayed his fingers along her stomach and rubbed the wave of lotion high up to her breasts.

"Kyle, please."

"Please what?"

Her eyes, round and dark and glittering with raw animal need, met his.

"Please now."

If he had been more of an officer and less of a man, he would have refused. But he had his needs, too.

He slid his body between her legs. And then remembered that the only thing he was leaving her was memories—not a child.

When he glided the sheath over himself, she shocked him by grasping his flesh.

"Let me," she said boldly.

The way her fingers trembled and struggled, he knew she hadn't done this before. And, in his urgent need, he nearly told her, "No, stop, I'll do it." But he used the pause in their lovemaking to remember that this time was about her. Not about him. He'd have plenty of women in his life—he had always been lucky with ladies, maybe too lucky. He could walk off the plane when it reached Sri Lanka, snap his fingers and have what he wanted. Whatever he wanted.

Kate didn't look like the kind of woman to snap her fingers. Kate was a proud woman—proud in a good way—and it would be a long time, perhaps a lifetime, before she'd let another man in her bed.

"Did I put it on right?" she asked, leaning back, her hair like a billowing cloud of red upon the pillow.

He checked. "Just right, Kate."

She surprised him a second time with her boldness by guiding him into her. He felt the hot, wet womanhood and it was all he could do to stop himself from taking his pleasures immediately.

He'd never left a woman unsatisfied, but then, he'd never made love to Kate. He wanted this to be special, perfect; he wanted this to be everything for her.

He moved gently against her, straining against her center of sensation, calibrating his movements to maximize her pleasure. He looked into her face. She matched his with a steady gaze.

He thrust, long and deep, and a soft moan escaped from her parted lips. Her head reared back and her eyelids fell. Her hair moved like molten copper on the pillow.

And then she began to move against him, drawing her legs up to bring him farther into her.

"Kate, I'm not going to be able to last much..."

Her eyes flew open, and the dark centers receded until all that was left was a sapphirelike blue. Surprise and fear and yet, a stunning, glittering trust, was there for him. She bucked against him, he protested again, and then suddenly she started to cry out.

He clamped his hand over her mouth, thinking of the noise she was about to make.

She trembled with fear, but he soothed her.

"It's all right, Kate, it's all right. I just didn't want you to wake the whole house up."

Her eyes met his, trust melting her fears.

Her hips heaved against him once again and he felt the concentric circles of her orgasm. Her face glowed, her eyes widened and she moaned against his palm.

The last conscious thought he had before he lost control was that she was the most beautiful woman he had ever met, freckles and all.

"I GUESS I AM the kind of woman who makes a lot of noise," Kate admitted. She snuggled against Kyle.

She had never felt so calm, so at peace, so fulfilled.

She wouldn't think about tomorrow.

"If I hadn't put my hand on your mouth, you would have woken up the Cabots," Kyle said. "They would have had the Winnetka police department in here within seconds. That Officer Bob who directs traffic would have drawn his gun and shot me dead."

"No, the Cabots wouldn't have called the police."

"Oh, yeah? And why not? Having you up here screaming might be cause enough."

Kate sat up and smiled smugly. "The Cabots are playing bridge next door with my parents," she said. "The house is empty."

Kyle's face registered surprise and then sly delight.

"How long do they play bridge?"

"Hours and hours."

He stretched like a contented lion and reached for the nightstand. He held out the bottle of lotion.

"Well, then, Kate, I think it's your turn to give me a back rub. I guess this time you can make as much noise as you want."

Chapter Fifteen

To the rest of Winnetka that morning, Kate was sure she projected her normal air of competence and sensibility. Certainly, if anybody had expected her to retreat into her home for a cry after the abrupt end of her engagement, they were surprised and mistaken.

But then, Kate had always put the needs of others before her own. And Winnetka's needs didn't go away simply because her wedding was canceled.

Dressed in a blue-and-white striped shirt dress, she attended the high school's English departmental breakfast meeting to discuss the coming fall semester, scheduled more volunteers to man the blood drive booths for Saturday and posted a flyer on the locker room announcing three more practices in anticipation of the Friday-night game against the Wilmette Huskies.

And yet, inside she carried a secret, a secret she knew she could never share.

She could hardly imagine what the friends and family she saw in the morning would think if they

knew that Kate had just risen from Kyle's bed. The
bed that used to be Parker's.

Kate herself wasn't sure what she thought.

Her world, her point of reference to all that she
cared about, was altered. She smiled. Yes, the satisfied smile of a sexually knowing woman.

But she also felt deep loneliness. Surrounded by
people who loved her and needed her, called friend
by so many, she was suddenly made aware of how
very much alone she truly felt.

Now that Kyle was gone.

She only hoped that the vividness of her feelings
would fade with time, but that her treasure—the
memory of his touch—would be untarnished.

He had been driven to the airport in the early
hours, by Mr. Nilson himself. She had watched the
cab glide down the street until it disappeared.

AT THE AIRPORT, Kyle found out he had been
bumped from stand-by and couldn't get a flight until
the next day. Paul Nilson drove him back to Winnetka and silently dropped him off at the Community House where Kate's meeting was in progress.

Kate nearly cried when she saw him, but she kept
a pleasant smile on her face as she expressed her
astonishment that the airlines couldn't be more ac-
commodating to a soldier returning to his unit.

Kyle accompanied Kate for the rest of the morning, saying that he was sure she wanted to keep any
eye out on him.

He could have stayed home—at the Cabots'

house. She trusted him to preserve Parker's reputation.

It was her reputation that was now of more concern.

What would her neighbors, her colleagues, her fellow residents of Winnetka think if by a single word or action Kyle gave away their intimate secret?

But though they had only hours before touched and caressed each other in every indecent manner possible, his demeanor was that of a perfect best friend of the hero. He never touched her, never looked at her suggestively, never winked or talked in double entendres that might give them away.

At first, Kate was baffled and hurt that he didn't acknowledge how much they had shared. Then she realized her gratitude—he knew small-town folks can read the nuances of a lingering glance or a hand brushing against a beloved's fingers as easily as they can their morning newspapers.

"You two are so good for each other," Mrs. Henderson, the next-door neighbor, said when they came home for lunch as she was watering the zinnias that bordered her lawn.

Kate's heart galloped.

How did Mrs. Henderson know?

"You're both in mourning for Parker," she said. "I think the lieutenant is showing wonderful devotion to his comrade by staying so long to comfort you. Don't worry, Kate, one day you'll have a man and you'll experience..." Mrs. Henderson blushed. "Well, all the things that I shared with my late husband, Colvin. You know, sensual things, marriage things, things a girl like you wouldn't know anything about. You just be patient. There'll be another man for you someday. My cousin Irma got married for the first time when she was in her fifties. It could still happen to you.''

Actually, there was a man right here, right now, Kate thought, touching her cheeks to see if a hot blush had developed.

But no, she was becoming as good at hiding her feelings as Kyle was.

The night before, she had turned her back on all that was sensible, dignified and responsible. She had become a wanton, an adventuress, a siren.

And, as she watched Kyle stride up to the Lodge house where her mother would serve them lunch, Kate knew she would do it again. This very night, if given the opportunity.

She walked into the house and brazenly offered her parents four tickets to the Ravinia outdoor concert for that evening. She had bought them at the Community House ticket counter twenty minutes after Kyle was dropped off by Mr. Nilson.

''What a wonderful surprise, Kate,'' her father said, pulling out his reading glasses to study the tickets. ''I see there's four of these. Would you and the lieutenant like to go with us? Might perk your spirits up, Kate. And, lieutenant, it might be a nice way of seeing more of what our town has to offer.''

''Oh, no, sir,'' Kyle said, staring at his sandwich rather than meet Kate's father's eyes. ''I'd better turn in early tonight. I'm pretty tired. And the flight tomorrow will be grueling."

"Oh, and I can't go. I have lesson plans to review," Kate added. She looked down at her plate. "Maybe you'd like to take the Cabots. You know, like you usually do. Besides, it's barbershop-quartet music. You know how much the Cabots like barbershop."

"Excellent idea," her father said, putting the tickets into his shirt pocket. "And I think we'll treat them to dinner at Irv's Diner afterward."

"But if we do that, we won't get back until long after midnight!" Mrs. Lodge protested, taking off her apron and sitting beside her husband. "Are you sure you want to be out that late?"

"I think it would be kind of fun," Mr. Lodge said. "And you won't mind, Kate, if we stay out late tonight, would you?"

"Of course not," Kate said smoothly and guiltily. "I'll be just fine."

"YOU MANAGED THAT with your usual trademark efficiency," Kyle said as they got into her car to drive to practice. "Well-done."

Kate startled, wondering if she was being too brazen, too presumptuous, too...easy.

"Kate, you don't need to play hard to get," Kyle said, as if reading her thoughts. "You've already got me. At least for tonight."

Kate turned on the ignition.

"And I want to make love to you tonight," he said. "More than one time. More than ten times."

"Kyle, that's impossible."

"Let's find out," he said with a boyish grin.

Her smile felt like it began at her toes and went through her whole body. She wanted to throw her arms around him and kiss him, really kiss him. And then ask him to show her more, more of the sensual pleasures she had only dreamed about until last night.

But Kate was still Kate. Mrs. Henderson was watering her flowers and would be only too happy to gawk at such indecent behavior as a kiss in the Lodges' driveway. There were other neighbors, behind lace curtains and damask drapes, who would see and comment and know. And get on their telephones with the scandal.

Besides, she'd scheduled a practice for the team this afternoon and Kate was not going to be late a second time to a practice. It would set a bad example.

And one thing that Kate would never be was a bad example!

So she let her private smile deepen and fill her body. And change from red hot to warmth, a restless but pleasurable warmth that settled at her belly and made her tingle with anticipation.

Six hours until the barbershop-quartet concert began, she thought. A virtual eternity.

"Ready, Miss Lodge?" Kyle asked.

He was inches from her, in the passenger seat of

her compact car. She could smell the faint masculine musk, and the sleeve of her warm-up jacket nearly touched the bare muscle of his own. But he was a model of decorum, his steel-blue eyes trained on the horizon ahead.

"Yes, Lieutenant, I'm ready," she answered crisply. "Let's get to practice."

HE WOULD HAVE TO GET on that plane tomorrow, Kyle thought as they drove to the high school. He could have gotten on this morning's plane, if he had said he was needed back in Sri Lanka. Airlines always accommodated soldiers that way. Or maybe he had always been good at charming ticket agents.

But he hadn't protested a bit when he was told the plane was full, and as he'd watched the plane leave the tarmac, he'd had a funny feeling of relief. Paul Nilson, apparently possessing some sixth sense, was waiting for him on the curb and drove him back to Winnetka. Depositing him without a word at the Community House, as if he knew all along where Kyle wanted to end up.

Kyle had to get on that next plane.

He told himself that he was acting like a gentleman, that it would be wrong to lure Kate into a night of passion and then run out on her the very next morning. Even if she had thought she understood how one-night stands operated, Kyle knew that her inexperience made her vulnerable.

Left alone the morning after, she would think she had acted unwisely, even wrongly, and she would regard his leaving as a sign that she wasn't a richly desirable woman.

But she was.

He told himself that it was his responsibility to reassure her—that while she had been the one to cross the arbor, it was he who had guided them further into the realm of the senses. Instead of seducing her, he could have sent her home with a long, lingering kiss and a regretful sigh. But he had given her every pleasure and had taken all that she gave. And she gave all of herself, with the innocence of a young girl and the intelligence of an older woman.

He had broken every rule he lived by. He couldn't, just couldn't, leave her the morning after. At least, he told himself, it was his personal sense of honor that propelled him back to the small town in the middle of corn land.

But he'd have to leave. Tomorrow morning. Tonight would be their last night together. He'd somehow have to explain all the reasons why he could never stay. Why he could never ask her to go with him.

He wasn't that kind of man. Wives and families and love for all time—protecting that stuff for other men was why he put his life on the line. But he knew it was never for him.

And she wasn't the kind of woman who could follow him, especially without a ring on her finger. She wouldn't leave Winnetka, wouldn't leave the people who depended on her so much, wouldn't leave for nothing more than the kiss of a rogue soldier.

He knew he couldn't ask, wouldn't ask. He knew she wouldn't follow him.

And he knew that even though he wanted her desperately, surprisingly so considering that she wasn't his type at all, he would get over her. Someday.

She had to do the same.

She had to find another man, had to have children, had to make her own family. Because she was a woman who was made to be a wife and mother. She had that much love in her, ready to give.

He began to speak as she pulled into the parking lot of the high school. "Kate, you understand—"

"I understand completely," she interrupted. "You're just here for tonight. Don't worry, Kyle, I want you on that plane tomorrow morning. No excuses."

"And I want you in my bed tonight."

She opened her mouth slightly and then her lips curved into a sly smile. Maybe she understood more about a brief affair than he thought.

"But, of course, Lieutenant," she said.

As she pulled into the parking space, he wondered how he would control his lust for the next six hours. He had never had to wait for a woman before Kate.

Though he ached in his loins, it felt good to wait.

"DARLING, this morning you really do have to get on that airplane."

She had said the same thing every morning she

had awakened in his arms. And every morning there had been some reason why he had to stay.

She pulled herself out of his drowsy embrace, pushed the purple and white Winnetka Central pom-poms off the pine chest at the end of the bed, and sifted through the pile of her clothes beneath.

"Can't leave today," Kyle murmured groggily. "Isn't the blood drive today?"

"Yes, it is."

"Then I have to stay until tomorrow. Can't let people down. Especially since we don't have Parker. I'd feel, like, really terrible if I let everyone down."

Kate pulled on her shorts.

He rolled over and buried his head under the pillow.

"For somebody who hates being here, you seem to have a lot of trouble going." She reached over and yanked the pillow from his head. With lightning speed, he whirled around and grabbed her wrists, playfully pinning her down on the bed beneath him. She giggled—but softly, careful not to wake the Cabots.

He kissed the base of her throat. "Don't worry, Kate. I want to get out of Winnetka as badly as you want me to."

The teasing fell flat.

Kate saw the shadow passing over his face and she looked away. To the nightstand. To the open bottle of champagne and the two fluted glasses. One with a pale, glossy lipstick imprint. The bubbles were gone, the glasses half-full. But they hadn't needed much champagne last night.

The first victory of the Winnetka Central High School Wildcats against the Wilmette Huskies had been only one reason to celebrate. Kate and Kyle had been making up other reasons to celebrate in each other's arms for four days.

Kate wondered how her family and friends would react if they knew that she was leading a double life.

Responsible, sensible Kate by day.

Sensual, sexually awakened Kate by night.

He showed her new ways to bring them both pleasure. He taught her sensual moves she hadn't imagined. She wasn't surprised at his knowledge of sexual technique, but she had been shocked at how adventurous she became. She did everything with enthusiasm and gusto, leaving her shyness and decorum on the windowsill.

Maybe it was because she knew she'd never see him again that she felt comfortable—no, thrilled—to try everything. To explore all the possibilities. To give herself up to making love and then surprise herself that there was no shame, no embarrassment, no barriers in sexual surrender. Nothing shameful about it. She was just...good in bed.

Good with the man she loved. Because she did love him with all her heart.

She was careful to keep that single secret from him, although they talked about everything else in the hours of night when they were sated.

He told her about his childhood in Kentucky,

about growing up on the wrong side of the tracks. Of not knowing his father. Of him and his mother making due on cocktail waitress tips. Of feeling restless and confined by the small town rules. Of feeling shut out of his own family when his mother remarried.

He had signed up for the army as soon as he'd graduated, and he had traveled the world. But he hadn't seen the sights that the tourists usually take in. In London, he rescued an American diplomat from IRA terrorists, but never got a chance to see Buckingham Palace. In South America, he led a raid on a drug cartel laboratory, but never saw the mountain area's ancient temple ruins. In Nepal, he foiled a kidnapping of American tourists by Kashmir separatists, but did not linger to appreciate the beautiful icy lakes and majestic mountain waterfalls.

And sometimes he grew anxious, trembling with the fear that he suppressed so completely on the field of battle. She soothed him, and knew that he resented that she had the power to soothe. He didn't want to depend on a woman. Any woman.

She listened to his stories as she lay in his arms, and she knew she couldn't tell him of her love for him. He would feel burdened by it, he would sear himself with guilt for having seduced her, and—worse—he would think she wanted to trap him into a life that he had long ago rejected.

She loved him too much to do that to him.

And while her heart went on a roller-coaster ride of despair and ecstasy as he prepared to leave and then ended up staying, she didn't mind. She was grateful for every single memory that she would have to keep.

After the night her parents and the Cabots went to Ravinia for the barbershop-quartet concert, Kyle said he wanted to help her team with its football practice just one more day. He worked those boys hard, but they loved it, and towards the late afternoon, Kate began to believe they had a better than even shot at beating Wilmette's team.

The morning after that, Kate's father asked if Kyle would stay to chop wood for Mrs. Sorenson who was elderly and whose children lived in Cincinnati and didn't know that she relied on her wood-burning stove during the cold months.

When Kyle finished chopping Mrs. Sorenson's wood, Mrs. Patton walked over from her house and asked if he would mind regrouting the tile in her bathtub because her husband was arthritic.

Then the Swifts had a sparrow's nest fall from beneath their porch eaves, and two baby sparrows had survived. Kate and Kyle nursed the tiny ones— feeding them sugar water every hour from an eyedropper until the animal hospital in Evanston took them. Kyle said he couldn't leave unless he knew that Pete and Chip, as they had named the two sparrows, would live.

The days filled up quickly with odd jobs and important deeds—the things Kate was used to doing all the time but that somehow had new excitement breathed into them.

The nights were devoted totally to the senses, with lovemaking that lasted 'til just before dawn. Kate had no idea where Kyle got his stamina with only an hour or two of sleep.

She herself had fallen asleep during the blood drive committee meeting she had chaired on Wednesday and had dozed off at her desk while developing lesson plans for the classes to start in September. And her eyes had developed the delicate shadows of sleeplessness. Mrs. Cruikshank took her aside at the hardware store one afternoon and said she looked as though she was holding up as well as she could but that she needed some rest.

It took Kate several seconds to realize that the mayor's wife was talking about Kate being dumped by Parker.

Her time with Kyle would come to a stop. She knew it would. And then she'd have her wrought-iron single bed to be alone in. But though she couldn't think of a time she wanted him to go, she knew it had to end. Soon.

She couldn't live a double life. Even aside from the fact that she needed a good night's sleep, she wasn't built for deception. And though it wasn't anybody's business but her own, she didn't feel comfortable with keeping secrets.

Or having an illicit affair.

The worst, though, was the daydreams she caught herself having. The ones where he stayed and they built a life together. A wedding, a house, children, all the things a woman wants with the man she gives her heart to.

This morning, she asked him about his plans.

She hadn't wanted to ask, but she had to.

"Do you have work to do back home?"

"Home? Sure," he said without opening his eyes. "But I'm at the end of my enlistment. I haven't yet signed the paperwork for the next two years."

"But you're going to," Kate supplied neutrally. She wouldn't fool herself. He wouldn't stay. He would go back to Sri Lanka and join up again. He wasn't the kind of man who wanted a small town, a wife or a white clapboard house with a picket fence.

"Of course, I'm going to reenlist," he said. He opened his eyes and stared at her thoughtfully. "Kate, this is hard for you, isn't it?"

Her throat caught. "Yes," she admitted. "Yes, it is. The longer you stay, the more I want you to stay. For good."

"Kate, I didn't make any promises."

She shook her head. "I know you didn't. I've known that all along. I wanted something from you. A memory to cherish forever. You've given me that. But, Kyle, if you're going to go, you'd better go soon. Before it gets too hard for me to say goodbye."

He reached out to her, but she eluded his grasp and he was good enough at reading her body that he knew she didn't want him to touch her now. She dressed, pulling on her bra and shirt with her eyes averted. She hadn't felt modesty since the first night, but now she felt her nakedness acutely.

Just as she was easing the window open, there was a knock on the door.

"Lieutenant?" Mrs. Cabot called.

"Uh, just a minute, Mrs. Cabot. I'm not dressed," Kyle answered.

He slipped noiselessly from the bed and splayed his fingers gently on the door ready to put his full weight on it if Mrs. Cabot tried to enter. Kate's heart caught.

"Lieutenant, I've just got to tell you!" Mrs. Cabot called from the hallway.

"What is it?"

"I have great news! Parker's home!"

Kate felt her legs go weak.

"That's…that's wonderful, Mrs. Cabot," Kyle improvised. "He's here now?"

"Yes, he just got in. Said he couldn't bear to have hurt poor Kate. He hasn't said so, but I'll bet they're going to get married now and live happily ever after right here in town! It's just like what we always dreamed of for those two."

Kyle stared at Kate, and they both remembered what had brought them together. And what would tear them apart.

"Tell Parker I'll be down in a minute," Kyle said.

He waited until Mrs. Cabot's footsteps faded, and then he took his hands from the door. He looked at her. Kate waited, he knew, for the words—any words—that would tell her that she was his woman.

But he didn't say anything.

It was the quiet that shamed her. "You're an honorable man," she said at last.

A pained expression crossed his face, but he didn't say anything to refute her. He wouldn't make promises he wasn't going to keep. He protected the innocent—but thought love, family and community were for other men. He wouldn't take a buddy's girl.

He wouldn't say the words *I love you* unless he meant them. For always.

Yes, he was an honorable man.

Kate knew that right now he thought he had dishonored himself by taking over, however briefly, the life and the woman that should have been Parker's.

But whether honorable or not, he didn't do the one thing that would prove his love—he didn't ask her to stay.

With his silence ringing in her ears, she pulled up the window and climbed onto the arbor to her own bedroom window.

Chapter Sixteen

When she crawled back into her bedroom, her mother was frantically pounding on her door.

"Kate! Kate! The most fantastic news!"

Though her heart was breaking, Kate kept her expression steady. She opened the door.

"Yes, I can guess," she said listlessly. "Parker's back."

Her mother bustled past her and flung open Kate's closet. "I've already called Mrs. Maguire," she said, rummaging through the hangers. "We have to find that dress! He's back just in time for the wedding tomorrow."

"Wedding? Tomorrow?" Kate asked with a creeping sense of horror.

"Don't you remember, darling? Your wedding was scheduled for tomorrow. Parker came back just in time—he must have realized that even with his job on the Special Forces he could still marry."

Kate stared at the floor.

Her mother glanced back at her daughter.

"You run along and go see him. I'm going to

find that wedding dress. Mrs. Maguire thinks she can stitch it up overnight. Oh, and I've got to call that caterer. And the florist still hasn't sent those roses to the seniors' home, so…''

Her mother suddenly looked back at the bed. Smoothed quilt. Plumped-up pillows. Sheets tucked under the mattress.

She regarded her daughter carefully. Denim shorts and plain white T-shirt. The same outfit she'd been wearing the night before. The eyes delicately shaded from a sleepless night, but glittering with heightened emotion.

''I got up early,'' Kate lied.

Her mother stared at the bed for several long moments. And then she asked an unexpected question.

''But, Kate, why was your door locked? We don't even lock the bathroom door in this house.''

''Mom, don't ask me.''

''Kate, we've always been close. Can't you tell me what's going on?''

Kate shook her head. She couldn't say. She knew her brief affair with Kyle would have to remain a secret. Even from her mother, with whom she was ordinarily very close. But if she told her mother, the truth would upset the delicate balance of the friend-ship between the Lodges and the Cabots.

She would rather be silent than harm the two cou-ples.

''Darling, sometimes you have to choose between duty and happiness,'' her mother said softly. ''You were always the best little girl, and you've grown to be a wonderful woman. You've always chosen duty. But when it comes to matters of the heart, you need to choose your happiness. No one wants you to be unhappy.''

"Mother, there is no choice," Kate said firmly.

"Kate, there are always choices."

Shaking her head, Kate turned away from her mother and woodenly walked down the stairs. She felt a weight upon her chest. She really had no choice—she had a family to care for.

But what would she have done if Kyle had asked her to go with him? She couldn't say and she supposed the answer didn't matter. He hadn't asked, and while her heart would choose to follow him to the ends of the earth if that's where he happened to go, her head had a firm grip on the hopelessness of the situation and on her duty to family, to friends, to community.

She trusted her mother to never ask her again, although she was sure that her mother knew without any doubts what had been happening every night.

She paused at the bottom of the stairs, thinking of that first moment when she had seen him. He had stood right there, next to the grandfather clock.

Would she think of Kyle every time she came down these stairs? Or would the memory fade, 'til all she had was the lilac bloom pressed between the pages of her Bible?

She took a deep breath, gulping back the emotion, as she opened the front door.

She felt like Kate again—and knew that the past

days she had let a part of herself develop that would now have to be put aside.

Put in a special part of heart labeled Private.

She was Kate Lodge. Sensible, dependable, responsible Kate. Nothing selfish, wanton or pleasure seeking about her. Nothing like a woman in love.

She opened the screen door and stepped out onto her family porch.

The Cabots stood on the lawn. Parker was tall, ruddy-faced and golden-haired, wearing a pink polo shirt and matching plaid shorts. He glowed, as always, with affability and charm.

Kate waited for the little skip in her heart that had always come, had been there from the moment they had decided to marry. It didn't happen, and then she knew for certain that she would stand fast.

Even if all of Winnetka were counting on her.

Even if her family was depending on her.

Even if Parker was relying on her.

Just this once, she'd have to let them all down.

In just this one little way.

She'd be a spinster. And she could never explain to people why she had made that decision.

He stopped in the middle of telling a joke to his parents when he saw her.

"Kate!"

He strode over to the Lodge front porch, took the steps two at a time and put his arms around her stiff, cold body.

"Oh, Kate, it's so good to see you," he exclaimed. "My parents say that you've taken such good care of them. Thank you."

"No problem," she said reflexively, pulling away from his embrace.

Out of the corner of her eye, she saw her father's car back out of the driveway with Kyle in the passenger seat. Kyle leaned out the window as her father paused at the curb.

"Is this goodbye?" Kate asked, hoping the trembling in her voice wouldn't give away how she felt.

"Yes…Miss Lodge…I'm afraid it is," he said. "I have taken advantage of your hospitality for too long but I hope you will forgive me."

She looked at the Cabots and at Parker. And she knew that Kyle was doing everything he could to protect her reputation.

Kyle had never touched her in public, never made any acknowledgment that there was anything more than a cordial friendship between them. He wasn't about to trumpet their relationship now.

She couldn't make a scene. She could only keep her dignity. There would be no tearful, sentimental goodbye.

"Why, Lieutenant Reeves, it was our pleasure to have you," she said, with the calm of a veteran hostess. "Do call upon us again if you travel through Winnetka."

"I will, Miss Lodge. But if I don't, please know that I will always remember the kindness of this…town," he said. "Take care of her, Parker. And don't be fool enough to let her go."

With a similarly formal thank-you to the Cabots and a curt nod to Parker, he rolled up his car window and the sedan lurched out onto the street.

"See ya, Kyle!" Parker shouted.

Kyle treated him to a murderous look.

Kate watched the car until it disappeared, turning onto Provident Street.

He was gone forever. And all she had were memories.

She stood very silently and then became aware that the Cabots and her presumed fiancé, Parker, were staring at her expectantly.

"Um, Kate..." he said.

She had memories. And she had Parker to deal with.

"We have to talk," she said.

"We'll leave you two lovebirds alone," Mr. Cabot said, steering his wife back toward their home.

"MR. LODGE, I think the turnoff for the highway was back that way," Kyle said, as they crossed the intersection of Provident and Willow.

He pointed toward the rear window, but Mr. Lodge cheerfully continued on his way.

"I know, Lieutenant, I just wanted to take another gander at the football field. See, the boys are out practicing this morning. Kinda early, wouldn't you say? But they're definitely motivated now that they've got a win under their belts. Yep, they've got a definite swagger about them. Beating the Wilmette Huskies after all these years. Who would have thought? We all know who we have to thank for that.''

''Who?''

''Why, you. Of course.''

Mr. Lodge maneuvered the car up the gravel path to the field. The automatic sprinklers watered the grass in long, graceful arcs. The team, under the direction of its captain, was doing push-ups in the dew-drenched center field. Kyle watched and had to admit that the boys were working harder than they had when he first saw them. Although it was not yet nine o'clock, their faces were red and damp with sweat.

''Winnetka owes a great debt to you,'' Mr. Lodge said. ''You've made this team win. After such a string of defeats, this win against Wilmette was mighty special. The parents are proud. The school administrators are willing to fund another year of sports. The whole community's coming together in their support of the team. All because of you. Look at all that purple and white.''

Kyle glanced out the window.

At nearly every house facing the campus, some evidence of Winnetka Central spirit had been put out. Purple and white banners hanging from windows. Sheets with congratulations to the team scrawled on them were draped from porch eaves. One homeowner had spelled out GO WILDCATS on his lawn with his mower.

''We thank you,'' Mr. Lodge said quietly.

Kyle squirmed uncomfortably. He didn't like

hearing thank-you's any more than he liked the adulation accorded to heroes.

"You're most welcome, Mr. Lodge, but can we go to the airport now?"

"Sure. I forget, we've taken so much of your time already," Mr. Lodge said, easing the car back to the street. "A young man like you has probably got plenty of folks waiting for you. Things to do that need your attention."

Actually, Kyle didn't have anybody waiting in Sri Lanka, except maybe for a clerk with a reenlistment form for him to fill out. But he let Mr. Lodge's comment pass.

"A man like you has fought a lot of battles, seen a lot of combat, faced a lot of danger," Mr. Lodge mused. "That's what a hero is."

"I don't like to think of myself that way."

"Oh, but you should." Mr. Lodge chuckled. "You know, you'll think I'm silly, but I think there's another kind of hero, too."

"What kind is that, sir?"

"The kind that gets up every morning and works and takes care of his family and helps out all the good folks in his community." He slid into a parking space in front of the hardware store. "I like to think my little hardware store makes it possible for people to do what they've got to do. Keep the roofs over their heads, keep their children warm, make things run smoothly. So, in a funny kind of small-town way, I'm a hero."

Kyle shook his head. He knew where this conversation was heading, and he didn't like it. Not one little bit. "I'm not that kind of man, Mr. Lodge. Don't ever get me confused with someone else," he said. Then he added more harshly than he intended, "If you can't get me to the airport, I'll get out of the car right now and walk there myself."

"I'll drive right on through to the airport right now," Mr. Lodge promised good-naturedly, putting the car into Reverse.

Kyle nodded gratefully and pulled his aviator shades from his inside jacket pocket. He wanted to hide behind their unforgiving black lenses. He wanted to brood, he wanted to think about Kate, he wanted to wonder why he was the kind of man to walk away from a good woman, he wanted to wonder if he'd ever forget her.

"You're right that you're not the kind of man to stay," Mr. Lodge said quietly. "I never thought you were. You did seem awfully miserable this week."

"I wasn't miserable, sir."

"Really?"

Kyle thought about the week. He'd been hot, up on the Lodges' roof under the unforgiving sun. He'd been tired—so many late nights with Kate followed by packed days. Frustrated—if one other person walked up to him and said he must feel very honored to have served with Parker...well, he'd scream. He'd been bored—those library committee meetings could really drag on.

And he'd been tense—that game last night had

been a real nail-biter right up to when the clock ticked off the final seconds of the fourth quarter.

But miserable?

Never.

He had been ecstatic. He had been exultant. He had been happy. He had found love. He had fooled himself that he wanted to go, but then when he left her, he felt a pain as sharp and as sure as a bullet to his chest.

"Lieutenant, look!"

Kyle glanced up. "Yes, Mr. Lodge?"

"It's Mrs. Sorenson's house—look at all that wood piled up. You chopped enough wood so that she'll stay warm all winter."

"Sir, are we on the way to the airport?"

"Sorry, Lieutenant. I was sure you wanted to drive one last time past the library, seeing as you helped out on the committee."

"Not meaning any disrespect, but I'd just like to get to the airport."

"Of course, I understand," Mr. Lodge said.

Mr. Lodge swung onto Willow. After satisfying himself that his driver was navigating a course that would get to the airport, Kyle leaned his head back against the headrest, closed his eyes and thought of Kate.

He hadn't made any promises at all. And that should be enough for him to honorably turn his back and leave. It had worked with every other woman of his experience. Besides, she was going to marry Parker, wasn't she?

"You've had a lot of combat experience, right?"

"Uh, yeah," Kyle admitted.

"Fought for your country."

"Yes," Kyle said, trying to tamp down the note of annoyance in his voice.

"For honor and justice and democracy and freedom?"

"That's what soldiers are usually sent into the field for."

"Ever fought for something that was important to you personally?"

"Like what?"

"Like a woman."

Kyle swallowed. It was out in the open. "Mr. Lodge, Parker's back. They're getting married."

"How do you know?"

"Your families are all tied up with each other. I've seen this town for a week. It wouldn't work if I'm married to Kate."

Damn, Kyle thought, staring at Mr. Lodge with his mouth hung open. He'd said the word. The *M* word. Married. Married to Kate.

But that's where it was going. If he turned around and went back down the street into Winnetka, if he saw her one more time, that would have to be the promise that he would make. Anything less would be unfair to her. Anything less would not make her his own.

Married. Kyle Reeves married. Absolutely ridiculous. Out of the question. He was not husband material. He didn't depend on anyone for his life, wouldn't be tied down to anyone.

Mr. Lodge kept his eyes steadily on the road, appearing not to register Kyle's discomfort. "I've always thought Parker and Kate would have made a good brother and sister," he said quietly. "And if it's not married love, it's not going to work for either of them. As for you, young soldier, how long do you expect to be doing what you're doing?"

"'Til I die, sir."

"Awfully lonely life," Mr. Lodge mused. "Short one, too."

Kyle tugged at his tie, which felt more constricting than ever. He realized that he had never felt lonely—until Kate had taught him what it was like to not be alone anymore.

"Lieutenant, if you love my daughter, this is the time you have to fight for her. There's no other time in life for her. Or for you."

Kyle looked at the older man.

He had fought for democracy and honor and virtue. He had fought for countries he couldn't locate on a map until he was sent to protect their shores and their ballot boxes. He had rescued American citizens from all sorts of dangers simply because...because they were Americans, and being an American meant something. He had fought for his men whether he personally liked them or not—that's what honor was.

Kyle Reeves.

Married man.

Somehow the description didn't sound quite so ridiculous anymore.

"Mr. Lodge, turn the car around."

Mr. Lodge pulled an immediate U-turn. Cars in the westbound lane honked loudly. A driver in the eastbound lane made an obscene hand gesture. Mr. Lodge wished him a good day.

They made record time getting back to the house.

As the car slipped into the driveway, Kyle saw Parker and Kate talking in the backyard garden of the Lodge house. He hesitated. The couple was holding hands, their heads together as Kate was showing Parker the flowers.

Had they decided on marriage?

"Gotta fight for what you believe in," Mr. Lodge said with surprising mildness.

KYLE STRODE OUT onto the lawn.

"Hey, buddy!" Parker said in greeting. "Good to see you."

Kyle grabbed Parker with one strong, sure hand.

"Kyle, don't!" Kate cried in outrage.

"Stay out of this, Kate," Kyle ordered. "This is between me and Parker."

Parker hung his head, staring at the broad fist that gripped the front of his polo shirt.

"He's right, Kate," he said solemnly. "It's between him and me. I took his medals."

"But you can't hit him," Kate pleaded. "Not because he took the credit for your medals. He knows he's done wrong and he's going to apologize."

Kyle looked at his other hand, which had curled reflexively into a brawny, white-knuckled fist. He looked at Parker. Parker stared wide-eyed at the coming blow.

"This isn't for the medals," Kyle said to him. "And it's not even for sending Kate a letter—because it looks like you've apologized for that. And it's not for making me responsible for riding in your parade or giving your damn speech. And it's not even for leaving a whole town without its hero."

"Then what's it for?" Parker whined.

"It's for stealing...my girl."

Kate seized his fist.

"Of all the male chauvinistic notions I have ever heard coming out of your mouth! You can't steal a woman."

Wiggling out of Kyle's grasp, Parker tugged his polo shirt's collar back into place. Kyle dropped his menacing fist. But though he tried to hang on to Kate's hand, she slipped away. As her fingers left him, he suddenly realized what was missing.

Her ring.

Her diamond engagement ring.

She wasn't wearing it, and Kyle felt his heart beat loudly with pride and excitement. She no longer belonged to another man. She was his....

But he cautioned himself not to get too cocky because Kate had a funny way of surprising him. She wasn't like any other woman he knew, but she was the woman he had to have.

"Uh, Kyle, I haven't stolen her," Parker said,

with a nervous glance to Kate. "If women could be stolen, that is. I was just telling her I have to go back. And she's sending me back. She doesn't want to marry me anyhow."

Kyle's eyes narrowed. "You're going back?"

"I can't live here. I don't belong here. There's another Parker—the Parker every Winnetkan thinks he knows—that Parker belongs here. Not me. I belong in Sri Lanka. That's my home. I've built a life there based on who I really am. I'm known as a respected businessman there."

"You're known as a party boy."

Parker wagged his finger in Kyle's face. "Yeah, but a very respected party boy," he said. "By the way, you know that Chinese saying I told you about when you save somebody's life?"

Kyle groaned.

"Yeah, I remember."

"Well, I want you to release me."

"Release you?"

"Yes. I'm tired of belonging to you, of having to serve you for the rest of my days. I'm tired of being your servant. I want to be free. In exchange I'll give you this."

Parker held his hands high in the air, toward the Cabot house, the Lodge house, the valley leading to the shops of downtown Winnetka, to the village green and the high school.

His hands stretched toward the four corners of Winnetka, to the rolling cornfields that formed its western borders and the eastern shore of its cool, rippling lake.

"All this I give to you," Parker said. "All of it. All this in exchange for getting my life back. I can't be your servant anymore. It's too much hassle. Too much work."

"You've never been my servant and you've never done any..." Kyle growled. "Hey, what about Kate?"

Parker chuckled and sauntered away. "Winnetka I can give you," he called over his shoulder. "Kate you have to earn on your own."

Parker shrugged his polo shirt back into place and disappeared into the Cabot house.

Chapter Seventeen

Kyle waited until the Cabots' back screen door slammed shut. "Parker's got a positive talent for handing other people responsibility," he said dryly.

Kate nodded and turned away to look with apparent interest at the peonies. She felt uncomfortable and awkward and edgy in his presence.

Her heart had thrilled when she had seen him stride back onto the lawn. He had come back for her! And it was all she could do not to throw herself into his arms and kiss him.

But she had stopped herself, knowing as perhaps he did not, that their relationship could never work out. Theirs was made for memory.

She hoped the list of the responsibilities Parker had left her with would help Kyle to understand why she couldn't follow him to the ends of the earth. If he were asking...

She had to stay here. Too many people depended on her.

"I've sworn a solemn oath to care for his parents, my parents, the blood drive, the hardware store, the library board and the football team," she said, wondering if she had left anything off her list.

"What about you?" he asked at her shoulder. "Who's going to take care of you?"

"Parker knows I can take care of myself," Kate said, while inside she wanted to scream, to cry out, to at least show some pique.

Kyle was an honorable man, caught by two different choices—each honorable and dishonorable in its own way. He wanted to serve his country, but he didn't want to abandon her. He wanted to claim his woman—and the knowledge that he considered her his woman made her heart soar—and yet he couldn't quit the responsibilities of his job.

She loved him enough that she wouldn't spoil his choice. Because she had made hers.

Duty versus happiness, just like her mother said. For Kate, duty always won out.

"Can you truly, Kate?" he asked. "Can you take care of yourself?"

"Of course," she said, hoping she hit the right note of certainty and strength.

He pulled a key from his pants pocket.

"Because I have a little tea and cardamom plantation on the southern slope of Mount Pidurutalagal," he said. He didn't notice the glitter of tears welling in her eyes. "It's a small plantation, only employs about five hundred workers and houses about thirteen hundred. I don't get involved in the day-to-day stuff too much, but it's profitable and it has a large estate house."

Kate wiped a tear from her cheek. Dependable, no-nonsense, responsible Kate. Crying.

But she knew he had made his choice. To go back. And he was giving her the option to follow. But whether as a wife, a mistress or just a friend she occasionally made love to, she couldn't take it.

"Darling, what's wrong?" Kyle asked, grabbing her into his embrace.

And then it came. In great torrents. Tears and big, gulping sobs. Her shoulders trembling, her hands shaking as she batted his comfort away. She knew her cheeks were splotchy red and she needed to blow her nose. The deepest despair overtook her.

Here was happiness. Set against duty. Here was her one chance. And she would not, could not take it. She had made her choice—he had made his. They had both chosen duty.

He had simply thought he could have happiness on the side. But duty and happiness never really work out that way. *You have to choose,* Kate thought miserably.

"I can't go!" she cried out. "I just can't go."

Kyle fingered the key and knit his brows together. As he stepped back she thought she saw all her future happiness torn from her heart.

And then he took her hand, putting the key onto her palm.

She shook her head blindly.

"I can't go, I can't go," she murmured.

"Kate, Kate, listen to me," he said. "I'm not asking you to go anywhere. I was thinking we could sell this plantation—I don't drink much tea anyhow. And cardamom isn't my favorite spice.''

Kate gulped back another wave of sobs.

"Sell it?"

"Yes, and buy something a little more practical," Kyle said. "On the way back from the airport, your father showed me a nice little bungalow on Ash Street."

Kate blinked. "Ash Street?" she asked inanely, swiping the back of her hand across her wet face.

"Yeah, we want to stay in town," Kyle pointed out. "Darling, we have responsibilities. Parker's just given me the whole of Winnetka. I can't let him down. I can't let Winnetka down. Think of my duty. To your parents, Parker's parents, the hardware store, the football team, the blood drive, the library…"

Kate opened her palm and stared at the gold fili-greed key. "You'd give this up?" she asked tentatively.

He nodded. "It was never home, Kate. I've been fighting all my life—fighting for, and yet running away from a home that didn't exist. It's here, Kate. Because I love you it's here. And I don't have to fight, and I don't have to run. I just have to love you. I guess I've become one of those soldiers who have to go home."

He gestured around the yards that bordered the Lodges' home.

"It's all here in this small town, which is every inch yours," he said, looking over her shoulder and grimacing. "Oh, great, Mrs. Maguire is watching. She's going to fall out of that window if she leans any farther."

Kate turned her head. Mrs. Maguire waved from her bedroom window where she snipped at the weeds on her flower box. If the seamstress didn't put away those clippers soon, there wouldn't be any impatiens or geraniums left at all.

Then Kate's eyes caught sight of Mr. Nilson who had left his early lunch smoking on the barbecue as he stood blandly watching Kate and Kyle, his spatula in one hand and his soda can in the other.

She saw the Joyces' upstairs window curtain flutter suspiciously—surely that was Mrs. Joyce's face outlined on the screen. Tom Smith had been playing catch with his dog Spike but now he had abandoned the pretense of disinterest and was staring over the hedge, riveted to the unfolding drama. Mrs. Henderson watered her flowers mindlessly, eyes trained on the couple. Her hostas and tiger lilies were in danger of being washed away.

"Kate, if I kiss you now, it'll ruin both our reputations," Kyle said slyly. "We'll have to marry each other immediately. Tomorrow at the latest."

Marriage? To her own hero?

The happiness was almost too much to bear.

But she had chosen happiness and hadn't sacrificed her duty.

She looked at him with as much cool sophistication as she could muster. "I suppose you're right," she said. "It'll take about ten minutes for news of this romance to get all around town."

"Well, then, darlin'," Kyle drawled. "Let's really give them something to talk about."

He pulled her into his arms and gave her a long, slow, wet, lingering kiss, grinding his hips into hers until they both were sparked as surely as fireworks and pushing her skirt up with one hand so that his fingers splayed against her thighs.

As they lost their balance, falling into a giggling heap on the cool grass, Kate heard Mrs. Maguire cry out, "Oh my goodness!" Mrs. Henderson dropped her hose and screamed as the cold water ran over her shoes.

WHEN THEY WALKED hand in hand back to the house, Kate started to feel the familiar clutch in her throat. How would she explain...? Would her marriage to Kyle be upsetting to others...? Who would need to be comforted, who would need to be soothed? How could she explain what she had done?

She would have to bring the two families together and make her announcement.

She hoped for a moment or two alone with Kyle before she had to speak. She needed to compose her thoughts and her words carefully.

This was the kind of thing she really did need to write out index cards for. But instead of running for her desk, she put her hand into Kyle's firm grip and faced her family and friends head-on.

They found the three Cabots and her parents

seated at the kitchen table. All five stared open-mouthed at Kate and Kyle. Her mother and Mrs. Cabot held each others' hands—presumably for strength in this time of turmoil. Mr. Cabot peered over his spectacles owlishly at Kate as if he were just meeting her for the first time. And Mr. Lodge smiled the same way he did when he had the very best bridge hand. Parker looked oddly pleased.

"I told them," he said, rising from the kitchen table.

"What part?" Kyle asked, coming up behind Kate and putting his arms around her waist. His touch felt proprietary to Kate, but so strange after a week of keeping their distance in public. "And how much of it was the truth?"

"I told them everything."

"Everything?" Kyle challenged.

"And it was all true."

Mr. Cabot rose from his chair.

Mr. Lodge leapt up to help his friend, but Mr. Cabot batted his hand away.

"Son," he said to Kyle. "We've underestimated you."

"Yes, we have," Mrs. Cabot murmured.

"You saved our son's life," Mr. Cabot said. "And we thank you."

"And we'll give you back the medals," Mrs. Cabot said.

"I don't really want them," Kyle said.

"But they're yours."

"Throw them out. I've never liked medals."

He stared at Parker thoughtfully. "Does this mean I don't have to whip your butt?" he asked.

Parker's smile was boyish and affable. "Hey, pal, if you just asked Kate to marry you, this makes us brothers. Sort of."

"I have. But what's this about brothers?"

"Kind of brothers," Parker conceded. "And you know what the Chinese say about brothers, don't you?"

Kyle grabbed Kate's hand and headed for the door.

"No, Parker, and I don't want to know. Because I have a sneaking suspicion I'm not going to like it."

Parker grabbed his elbow. "The Chinese wise men say that the brother who's getting married should go and have a great day with his bride," Parker said. "And leave the wedding plans to me. I'll put together a party for tomorrow that'll even beat anything I've done in Colombo."

"Party planning is something you're actually very good at," Kyle observed.

Mrs. Lodge stood and took her daughter's arm. "Kate, you chose happiness," she whispered. "I'm so proud of you."

"Now get on out of here, you two," Mr. Lodge said, shooing them out the door. "Parker's got work to do."

Kyle led Kate out the front door.

"But I've got things I'm supposed to..." she sputtered.

At the porch, Kyle put his finger to her lips. She kissed the warm callused flesh. Hers. He was hers now.

"Kate, choose happiness for today," he said softly. "For all of today."

She looked at him, losing herself in the blue sky of his eyes. Happiness. It was there for her. And all along, she had thought that happiness was for others.

"Happiness," she agreed.

She kissed his finger again and again and then he put his lips to hers. It was just eleven o'clock. The sprinklers were running. The children were laughing. The neighbors were gawking.

And Kate and Kyle chose happiness and love.

PARKER DID A GREAT JOB. The wedding was the wedding of the decade. At least, by Winnetka standards. The *Winnetka Talk* sent a reporter and a photographer. The mayor offered the use of his home for a rehearsal breakfast and his Cadillac for the ride to and from the church. Mrs. Maguire was stitching the hem of the dress right up until the moment Kate walked down the aisle.

Within hours of the ceremony, a Lodge cousin claimed the dress for her own wedding planned for six months hence. The dress was considered quite lucky and was quickly scheduled to pass from bride to bride for the next several years.

There wasn't a dry eye in the church, which was packed—and so was the lawn out front where the vows were played on the loudspeaker.

The reception was held on the village green. The Winnetka Citizen's League organized a potluck supper because the caterer couldn't work with such short notice. The Winnetka Patisserie staff pulled a double shift so that the nine-tier cake could be baked overnight.

Parker made two kinds of punch—one with a kick and one with the pure flavor of the tropics. He arranged for the limbo contest, for Kyle's mother and stepfather to be flown in from Brownsville, Kentucky, and got Kyle a great deal on an engagement ring made with diamonds mined from the mountains surrounding Colombo, Sri Lanka.

Later that night, the fireworks that hadn't been used up on the Fourth were shot off by the volunteer officers of the fire department. The Boy Scouts performed a color guard parade and didn't drop any of the flags.

Everyone agreed the bride looked radiant, just like a princess. And the groom—most people made a point of shaking his hand and welcoming him to the community.

His best man, Parker, bought Kyle's tea plantation in Sri Lanka and was very relieved that everyone in his hometown loved him for who he was. And not for who he had pretended to be.

Winnetka was, after all, very forgiving of its sons and daughters. Small towns usually are.

AFTER A SHORT HONEYMOON, Kate and Kyle settled into a bungalow on Ash Street.

Kyle became head coach of the high school's football team, bringing the Winnetka Wildcats to the Illinois Championships that very year. He took over his father-in-law's hardware store and was named chairman of the blood drive.

Kate continued to teach right up until the day before their first anniversary. She awoke to a small, nagging backache, but being Kate, she still went to work. A woman in her condition would have been forgiven if she declined to take on lunchroom supervision, but Kate had made it a practice not to give in to her aches and pains. Still, when she went after school to watch her husband run practice, her plight could no longer be denied.

Her water broke just as she was calling Kyle off the field.

With precision born of training, Kyle commanded the two halfbacks to run up to Kate's office and get the overnight bag that she kept at the ready. He then gave his key ring to the right linebacker, and asked him to bring the car around to the field. And to the rest of the team, Kyle gave the instruction that they should continue to practice that last play until they got it right.

Then Kyle swept Kate off her feet as if the extra forty pounds on her frame were of no account. He carried her across the grassy field to the waiting car. It was only then, looking into the back of the car, at the seat they had bought in anticipation of their baby, that Kate broke down.

"I'm scared," she confessed, grateful that the

normally not-very-sensitive Wildcats had backed up a respectful twenty feet. "All those Lamaze classes and the tour of the hospital—they haven't done any good at all. I'm still scared."

"That's what I'm here for," Kyle said, snapping the seat belt over her stomach. "I love you and I'm married to you and this is what husbands are supposed to do."

During the next four hours he soothed and comforted, cheered and encouraged. And when Kyle, Jr. was placed into Kate's exhausted arms, the retired soldier stared in wonder at the mother, and the baby who bore his name. They had anchored him to a world that he had thought would never welcome him.

"I love you," he said.

She looked up at him with glittering eyes.

"I love you, too," she said.

"You saved my life, you know. I would have been a lonely old soldier if Parker hadn't given me that letter and I hadn't found you."

The nurse tugged at his sleeve.

"You've got five grandparents and an uncle outside," she said. "They want to know if they can see the baby."

"Five grandparents and an uncle?"

"Yes. Mr. and Mrs. Lodge, your mother and Mr. and Mrs. Cabot. And Uncle Parker."

"Tell them to come in," Kate said.

As the door swung shut behind the nurse, Kyle

asked Kate if she thought that her parents or the Cabots minded that she hadn't married Parker.

"Heavens, how could you still doubt their feelings for you?" Kate shook her head.

But all doubts were vanquished as little Kyle, Jr.'s grandparents, all five of them, and Uncle Parker came in to admire the baby. As the oohs and aahs reached a crescendo, Mr. Cabot clapped Kyle on the back and told him that General MacArthur couldn't have done a better job himself.

EVER HAD ONE OF THOSE DAYS?

TO DO:

☑ late for a super-important meeting, you discover the cat has eaten your panty hose

☑ while you work through lunch, the rest of the gang goes out and finds a one-hour, once-in-a-lifetime 90% off sale at the most exclusive store in town (Oh, and they also get to meet Brad Pitt who's filming a movie across the street.)

☑ you discover that your intimate phone call with your boyfriend was on company-wide intercom

☑ finally at the end of a long and exasperating day, you escape from it all with an entertaining, humorous and always romantic Love & Laughter book!

ENJOY
LOVE & LAUGHTER™
EVERY DAY!

For a preview, turn the page....

Here's a sneak peek at
Colleen Collins's RIGHT CHEST, WRONG NAME
Available August 1997...

―――――――――

"DARLING, YOU SOUND like a broken cappuccino machine," murmured Charlotte, her voice oozing disapproval.

Russell juggled the receiver while attempting to sit up in bed, but couldn't. If he *sounded* like a wreck over the phone, he could only imagine what he looked like.

"What mischief did you and your friends get into at your bachelor's party last night?" she continued.

She always had a way of saying "your friends" as though they were a pack of degenerate water buffalo. Professors deserved to be several notches higher up on the food chain, he thought. Which he would have said if his tongue wasn't swollen to twice its size.

"You didn't do anything...bad...did you, Russell?"

"Bad." His laugh came out like a bark.

"Bad as in *naughty*."

He heard her piqued tone but knew she'd never admit to such a base emotion as jealousy. Charlotte Maday, the woman he was to wed in a week, came from a family who bled blue. Exhibiting raw emotion was akin to burping in public.

After agreeing to be at her parents' pool party by

noon, he untangled himself from the bed sheets and stumbled to the bathroom.

"Pool party," he reminded himself. He'd put on his best front and accommodate Char's request. Make the family rounds, exchange a few pleasantries, play the role she liked best: the erudite, cultured English literature professor. After fulfilling his duties, he'd slink into some lawn chair, preferably one in the shade, and nurse his hangover.

He tossed back a few aspirin and splashed cold water on his face. Grappling for a towel, he squinted into the mirror.

Then he jerked upright and stared at his reflection, blinking back drops of water. "Good Lord. They stuck me in a wind tunnel."

His hair, usually neatly parted and combed, sprang from his head as though he'd been struck by lightning. "Can too many Wild Turkeys do that?" he asked himself as he stared with horror at his reflection.

Something caught his eye in the mirror. Russell's gaze dropped.

"What in the—"

Over his pectoral muscle was a small patch of white. A bandage. Gingerly, he pulled it off.

Underneath, on his skin, was not a wound but a small, neat drawing.

"A red heart?" His voice cracked on the word *heart*. Something—a word?—was scrawled across it.

"Good Lord," he croaked. "I got a tattoo. A heart tattoo with the name Liz on it."

Not Charlotte. Liz!

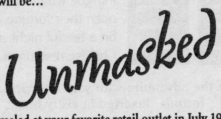

HARLEQUIN AND SILHOUETTE ARE PLEASED TO PRESENT

Love, marriage—and the pursuit of family!

Check your retail shelves for these upcoming titles:

July 1997
Last Chance Cafe by Curtiss Ann Matlock
The most determined bachelor in Oklahoma is in trouble! A lovely widow with three daughters has moved next door—and the girls want a dad! But he wants to know if their mom needs a husband....

August 1997
Thorne's Wife by Joan Hohl
Pennsylvania. It was only to be a marriage of convenience—until they fell in love! Now, three years later, tragedy threatens to separate them forever and Valerie wants only to be in the strength of her husband's arms. For she has some very special news for the expectant father...

September 1997
Desperate Measures by Paula Detmer Riggs
New Mexico judge Amanda Wainwright's daughter has been kidnapped, and the price of her freedom is a verdict in favor of a notorious crime boss. So enters ex-FBI agent Devlin Buchanan—ruthless, unstoppable—and soon there is no risk he will not take for her.

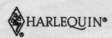 

HARLEQUIN®
AMERICAN ◆ ROMANCE®

LOOK WHO'S MATCHMAKING AGAIN!

By the time they were born—same day, same hospital, different parents—Malia, Chelsea and Garrett had already made sure they had both a mommy and a daddy there to greet them.

In 1995, Muriel Jensen brought you the stories you loved, the characters you laughed and cried with, in her bestselling series

mommy
+ me

Now return to Heron Point as
Malia, Chelsea and Garrett, now two years old,
face their toughest challenge yet,
in Mommy + Me's grand finale:

KIDS & CO. (#688)
by Muriel Jensen

Available in July wherever Harlequin books are sold.

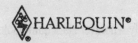